# deep waters

# deep waters

### a novel

## thomas eno

Covenant Communications, Inc.

Cover photo © 2002 PhotoDisc, Inc.

Cover design copyrighted 2002 by Covenant Communications, Inc.

Published by Covenant Communications, Inc.
American Fork, Utah

Printed in the United States of America
First Printing: June 2002

09 08 07 06 05 04 03 02    10 9 8 7 6 5 4 3 2 1

ISBN 1-57734-996-2

**Library of Congress Cataloging-in-Publication Data**

Eno, Thomas D., 1952-
    Deep waters : a novel / Thomas Eno.
        p.    cm.
    ISBN 1-57734-996-2
    1. Mormons--Fiction. 2. Illinois--Fiction. 3. Farm life--Fiction. 4. Floods--Fiction. I. Title

    PS3555.N65 D44 2002
    813'.54--dc21
                                                    2002023782

Dedicated to
the brave people of the Midwest
who gave all they had during the flooding of 1993
to preserve their lives,
and who showed the rest of us
what courage is.

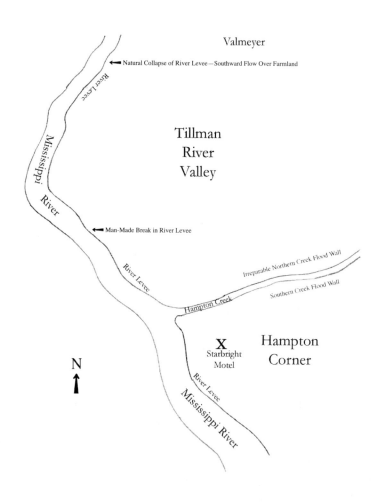

# prologue

Robbie MacFarland was alive. Really alive, as only the young can be. The day *belonged* to him. His heart was happy and free, his future bright and his dreams within reach. In fact, everything he saw was within his grasp.

Fingers tapping on the steering wheel, music from the dashboard radio filling the car, he flew along County Road 11 in his shiny, electric blue 1958 Ford pickup truck. His destination was the small town of Hampton Corner, but where he was headed didn't matter much. He was just enjoying every moment of life, wherever it took him.

Robbie had poured his heart and soul into his truck. What had been a rusted pile of junk was now his baby. From just a dream, countless hours of loving restoration had made it a part of him. And now he was driving the dream. As the truck flew effortlessly over the blacktop, Robbie flew too. He felt invincible, free, and immortal.

Robbie stuck his head out of the open window and swallowed mouthfuls out of the torrent of air that rushed by. It moved past him into the truck cab, and then out again through the sliding back window. The feeling was invigorating. The voice of his favorite country music star, George Strait, sang out of the radio. Snatches of song and the roar of the engine remained to sprinkle the landscape as the truck roared past.

He was feeling so *good.* His eyes glanced at the old-fashioned, awkward-to-adjust, lap belt laying unused on the seat of the truck. But his mother wasn't around, and she worried too much anyway. With a big grin he eased the truck single-handedly around a gentle turn in the road, thick trees flying by in a green blur.

Robbie dropped his right hand down from the wheel to steady the box beside him on the seat. Inside was a treasure, something wonderful for his younger, and only, sister Natalie. He anticipated her squeal of delight as the box opened, and there it would be. A genuine antique oil lamp. Natalie would be thirteen in a few days and was very much the dreamer. To her, writing by lamplight was a romantic idea and the way "real writers" wrote. She must have told Robbie a hundred times about the kind of hurricane lamp she wanted to own. Now the tall glass chimney and bowl stand would be hers.

Robbie smiled, enjoying the thought of surprising her.

Natalie was the family author. She had written her own (unpublished), full-fledged novel by the time she was ten. It was dedicated to Ray Bradbury, the author of *Dandelion Wine*. Natalie said his book was the most perfect novel ever written. Robbie had to take her word for it; he didn't read much.

But soon he would surprise her with the lamp. She would look so cute writing beside it—like a scene from a movie.

He smiled, causing his nose to itch. Rubbing first his nose, he followed the itch out to his freckle-covered cheeks—which the girls loved, guys kidded him about, and he tolerated—then his scalp. The last itch on his head attended to, he ran his fingers through his red, curly, untamably thick hair, a gift he inherited from his now-deceased biological father.

On impulse he again leaned his head out the window. When Robbie drove fast he always made a point of enjoying the rush of wind through his hair.

The country road was uneven, and right then the truck tires skidded over a large ripple in the pavement. But he didn't worry. Though there wasn't any power steering in the truck, he had rock-hard arms from hours of dedicated weight training and hard work on the family farm. So his right arm hung casually across the wheel, and his left rested, elbow first, out the window.

The road curved again, and his truck responded easily to his light touch on the wheel as he guided her through the tight turns. He was moving down the road at speeds far beyond the legal limits, and the weak spot on the bad, front left tire gave way a little more. The tire had needed replacing for months, but Robbie hadn't had the money to fix it. Other things had always come up.

It was 1991, the summer of his eighteenth year, and he was just a few months away from high school graduation. After that he would be off to Iowa State University to play football. True, he hadn't actually been signed up yet, but that would surely come before the end of this year's season. By then he would add a third All-State Wide Receiver award to the two other trophies on the mantle. His touchdown record, which would probably stand for a long time, was another reason a flock of college scouts descended upon his games.

Robbie smiled, thinking of the scouts; he enjoyed the attention. The scouts were always careful not to step beyond NCAA rules. Breaking the rules would make it impossible to sign him to their schools. But the rules got really hazy at times.

The truck's diminutive shadow showed it was late in that Saturday morning. The day was surprisingly cool for that time of year, but not as cool as it had been the night before. Robbie smiled and chuckled to himself.

Old man Fishel must have just about had a heart attack when he'd come out this morning and found that his VW Bug had been somehow picked up and set over the stone fence into his yard. Robbie and his buddies had done the prank to make up for the teacher's negative attitude toward them. The tight-lipped, skinny old crank had always been a pain, but lately he had turned into a nightmare. Fishel taught a required science course and enjoyed making the jocks sweat. He kept them in suspense until the last possible moment over whether they were going to be eligible to play. It was easy to dislike the man.

Robbie laughed again, reaching around to rub his lower back, thinking about what Fishel's face must have looked like. The Bug had been heavier than the guys had figured on and the stone fence higher. At one point the boys weren't sure if they could get it off the top of the fence where it had stuck. It had almost killed them to try and do it *quietly.*

*Maybe we should have left it teetering there,* Robbie thought. *That might have been funnier.*

Robbie was basically a good kid, he never did anything that damaged property or physically hurt anyone. The winter before he had actually gotten in someone's face to stop a prank that was getting out of hand. The other kids looked up to him as a leader, a role he wasn't completely comfortable with.

At that moment, as the speeding truck came round the next to the last bend in the road before the last miles to town, Robbie spied a lone figure walking along the side of the road. He slowed, looking. Although he was country-folk friendly, he had still been trained to be careful, so he slowed even more to eye the stranger.

The man was probably a drifter. Young looking, with longish brown hair but a clean-shaven face, the fellow wore sandals and brown pants and carried a denim jacket draped over his shoulder. Where had he come from? There weren't any deserted cars along the roadside, and it was five miles in one direction to Hampton Corner and a good twenty in the other direction to the last town, with nothing except farm fields in between. Robbie mentally shrugged and let it go, until a little voice inside nudged him, encouraging him to stop and pick the stranger up.

Reflexively, Robbie slowed, looking around in the truck cab. Had he really heard something?

Confused, Robbie pulled over to the side of the road and turned off his radio. The truck idled quietly as the man walked up alongside the truck. The two of them studied each other, but the man kept walking.

"Hey," called Robbie. "You need a ride?"

The man slowly stopped, turned, and returned to the truck. "That depends. Where are you going?" he asked, his voice low and gentle.

Robbie was struck by the calmness in the man's face. There was no sign of worry or anger, which most stranded motorists or hitch-hikers conveyed. This stranger was different. He seemed to have all the time in the world.

"I'm heading," Robbie put his arm out the window and pointed, "that way. Going into Hampton Corner. You're welcome to come along, if you want."

The man looked down the road he had been walking on, then back at Robbie. "Okay, I would be grateful for a ride. And you could use some company about now."

*Huh? I could use some company? He's definitely different,* thought Robbie, as he reached over and grabbed his duffel bag of workout clothes from the passenger side floor. Shoving it through the back window into the truck bed took some effort. "Door's unlocked," he grunted, as the man came around the front of the truck.

"I'm Robbie McFarland. You?" Robbie offered a hand shake as the man got in.

The stranger took the hand in his, grasped it firmly but did not shake it. "My name is John."

"O-kaaay." Robbie put the truck in gear. He couldn't say much for the guy's handshake, but he seemed harmless enough.

"Just passing through?"

John nodded. "I'm looking for work."

"What can you do?"

John shrugged. "Whatever I can. This and that."

Robbie rolled his head around to loosen his neck muscles. "Not much you could earn money from at our farm. My dad runs about three hundred hogs, not to mention too many acres of corn."

Glancing in his rearview mirror he drove on. "This time of year things get hopping. My dad depends on me a lot, but geez, I can't do it all. And my two little brothers aren't worth much, though I guess they try. My dad can be pretty hard to work for. Most everybody else likes him, though. I don't know, maybe it's just me."

By now, the bad tire had only a thin strip of rubber and steel holding it together, and it began to wobble slightly.

John smiled at Robbie understandingly. "Nice truck. Looks like you take good care of it."

Robbie tapped musically on the steering wheel. "The tires need replacing, but my dad said that will have to come later. I still owe him for the truck, and he's tired of waiting for me to pay it off. We had a big fight about it last weekend, and I gave him all the money I had just to get him off my back."

Robbie realized he was telling family things to a drifter, caught himself, and quieted. He was surprised how comfortable he felt with this guy when they hadn't even talked.

"The acorn seed," offered John, "can't grow in the shade of the tree it came from. It requires its own bit of sunshine, and rain."

Robbie looked sideways at John. He wasn't a brain like the guys in science class who sat around wondering why there was air, but he was keen enough to realize how the metaphor related. *Seed and tree? Seed and shade? Sunshine?*

"That's deep stuff. You a guru or something?"

Robbie passed a slow-moving motor home going determinedly up a hill in the opposite direction.

"No," answered John, smiling. "I'm only a man who also had a father."

Robbie nodded. "I get you. Guess it's pretty much the same all over."

They rode along in silence, until John touched the immaculate dash with care, then gestured to the car's expanse. "So, you did all this?"

Robbie regarded the car and John. "Yeah, it took me a lot of time. Looks good, don't it?" Then, as an afterthought, "How did you know?"

"There's a bond between you and the truck. When you touch it, you touch it with love."

Robbie laughed. No one had ever quite put it that way before.

The road dipped down and curved drastically to the right, putting an intense strain on the left tires. The weak area in the front one finally gave out, and the tire blew out with a bang. Terrified, Robbie fought to keep the truck under control, but it started fish-tailing over the road.

In a split second, the truck flew off the roadway and crashed into a stand of large trees nearby, the impact throwing the young driver through the windshield.

Moments later, except for the sound of the burning truck, all was still. John held Robbie's head in his lap beside the road, where he had carried him away from the burning truck. Robbie moaned, "I'm sorry, Dad. I'm really sorry. I promise I'll pay you back. I will."

John's eyes were wet with tears as he wiped blood away from Robbie's face. In a few minutes a car from town would be coming around the bend.

"It's all right," soothed John. "He loves you, Robbie. Your father loves you. It wasn't the money. It never was."

Laying his hands upon Robbie's head, John blessed him, and then carefully eased out from under the young man. Not a half second later, a maroon car came around the bend and quickly stopped as the driver saw the burning truck and the bleeding, unconscious boy alone by the side of the road.

# c h a p t e r   1

It was Saturday, the last day of July 1993, and John walked slowly along the Mississippi, following the river path near Hampton Corner, Illinois. Leaves whisked along in the currents, and the water lapped at places long untouched by the river. The river smelled of things and places far upstream; things alive and things decaying and dead. It smelled of hope, and it smelled of disaster.

About a month before, on the 26th of June, John had watched this same river in Minnesota. Up there it had flowed through St. Paul and crested more than five feet over flood stage. He had been in Clinton, Iowa, on the fifth of July, where the river rose seven feet over. And finally, on July 13th in Quincy, Illinois, the river crested fifteen feet over flood stage. Predictions for St. Louis, only fifty miles north of Hampton Corner, said the river would crest at twenty feet over flood stage on August 1st.

John tossed a stick out into the current and watched it move quickly downstream. The Gulf of Mexico was the river's ultimate goal, and it was heading there in a hurry. With each passing day the water climbed higher up the sand and gravel mounds that had always held it back.

He studied the thick, turbulent gray clouds overhead. They rose steeply and endlessly into the sky, higher and higher. Rubbing his neck with a sun-browned hand, he turned and squinted down at the river levee and the muddy, tumultuous rising water within. There wasn't much time left.

Water levels beside the levee changed constantly; that was the river's way. But this year was different. There was added water from weeks of rain in this unusually wet year, and it was creating something uncontrollably dangerous. This time John knew the river was going to beat the man-made wall that held it back. This time the river would once again prove it was untamable, far more powerful than those who strove to control it.

Coming around a bend, he came across a large, gnarled tree whose branches now hung closer to the water's edge than they once had—before the weeks of rising water. From a sturdy limb above John's head hung a thick rope with a crude wooden seat secured to the bottom. It swung invitingly in the humid breeze, the rope creaking slightly on the branch that bore its weight.

Here the riverbank was worn down from countless barefoot children who had come over the years to swing out over the water. A smaller rope, tied at the end of the large one, hung down into the river.

John could easily imagine a bright-eyed child pulling the large rope up the bank with the small rope. Then, settling securely on the seat, the child could push free of the earth and sail outward over the river and back. Larger kids probably stood as far back from the edge as they could, and then ran and jumped onto the seat. Likely more than once someone lost their grip and didn't quite make it, crashing into the water with a huge splash. Today the swing was abandoned. No one dared enter the flooding water.

Eyes twinkling, John hooked the smaller rope with a long stick and pulled the swing in. With a deep breath, he grasped the rope securely in his hands. Then stretching out his legs and breaking into a run, he careened down the bank and launched himself out over the water. His grip was strong enough to hang onto the rough rope, but he had to yank his legs up at the last moment to avoid hitting the water. The swinging rope underneath him dragged through the swollen river, leaving a small wake behind it as John's momentum carried him high above the water. He grinned fiercely, the air rushing through his hair and against his face.

Soaring to the top of his arc, John swiveled around and came hurtling back toward the bank. At the same moment, someone behind him and upriver called out for help.

John's concentration lapsed just long enough to throw his timing off, and he missed the moment needed to put down his feet and land. The rope carried him earthward, his forward momentum pushing him toward a rapidly advancing blur of greenery. Holding tight and yelping with surprise, he crashed into the barrier, landing in the middle of a thick patch of bushes and weeds. He moaned softly, mentally tallying his limbs. Was everything still there?

He blinked twice, spit out some dirt and leaves, and climbed gingerly out of the bushes. Large raindrops began falling, wetting his hair and face in a surprisingly short time.

"Help!" the call came again, louder and closer.

Now John could see far in the middle of the river. Someone was out there on a raft—or at least what was left of one. Whoever it was seemed to be more off it than on.

"Help me, somebody please!" came the wailing cry.

The cloudburst broke and John pulled off his sandals and dove into the river as the curtain of rain covered the land.

\* \* \*

The pouring rain and the river blended into a world of water. As John stroked powerfully out toward the middle, the Mississippi River tasted and smelled like wet newspapers, and worse. Now and then he caught a glimpse of the crumbling raft, but there was no clear sign of the person in danger. And no more calls either. John stretched out his arms, stroking and kicking powerfully, chasing the raft down the river.

After several long minutes the raft ran into a huge snag of trees and brush. The raft collapsed and disappeared underneath the snag. When John finally arrived, he dove into the water under it, gliding along like a dolphin. It was a dark mass of confusion; sticks, snags, branches grasping and tearing at him. He struggled, looking for a flash of color that would show him where the body he knew had to be there was.

Then he saw it, an arm thrashing wildly under some branches, its owner caught amidst the tangled mess beneath the water. John forced himself deeper under the morass, using the tangled branches to lever himself closer. Reaching out for the arm, he found a small boy at the end of it. The child's eyes were wide, full of terror, and frantic. The back of his pants were caught fast in the branches.

John thought he had pulled away enough from the deadly flotsam to give him room to safely work the boy loose, but suddenly the snag rolled in the water's current, hooking John's leg in the branches.

The boy's air was gone. Water filled his lungs, his eyes glazed over, bubbles poured from his mouth and nose.

John struggled frantically to pull both the boy and his leg out, to no avail. And then his air was gone too.

The boy's eyes closed and he stopped struggling and went limp.

*Why should the child die today?* prayed John. *Is it really his time?*

Focusing with all his might, he commanded the snag to let go of them.

A moment or two passed before a short vibration shook the two of them free. Gasping for air as he surfaced, John began the slow struggle back to shore, the limp body of the child cradled in his arms. Feet dragging, he finally brought the two of them ashore. The boy was dead.

John sank to his knees beside the body. Closing his eyes, quieting his mind, John could see a vision of the boy's mother in town, could feel what the loss of her only child would do to her heart and spirit. *Dear Father, this woman so needs this boy. Won't Thou spare his life for her?*

Laying his hands on the boy's head, and whispering words of faith and hope, he commanded life to return.

The boy's eyes fluttered, and then he spit up river water, coughing and choking. John helped him sit up and thumped him on the back, helping the boy catch his breath.

As the boy looked blearily at his rescuer, John said, "Hey sailor, what's the deal?"

"It looked like emeralds."

"What did?" asked John.

"The bottom of the river. It looked like emeralds."

John chuckled. "I was worried for a moment that you were going to stay down there permanently."

The child sighed, looking deeply into John's eyes. Then he looked back at the river, flowing along without care for the recent drama it was responsible for. The boy frowned and shuddered, "Me too!"

* * *

John accepted another chocolate chip cookie from the boy. "These are good." The boy was doing much better. His cheeks were beginning to regain some color, and he had walked quite steadily as he guided John back to his "hideout." For a while, John was worried the boy had swallowed the whole river and might suffer some serious side effects. But so far, so good.

The two of them were sitting inside a makeshift hut that the boy had constructed of bits and pieces of wood and tin over a few months. The pouring rain showed no sign of letting up, creating puddles here and there inside the shelter. At least the fire in the tiny, boy-scout-style fire pit kept them warm. Their wet shirts hung from sticks near the fire. "Did your mother make these cookies?" asked John.

"Nah," answered the boy, through a mouthful of cookie. "Charlene made these. She's a better cook than my mom. Heck, I bet Charlene's a better cook than *anybody.*"

"Is Charlene your sister?"

The boy shook his head. "Nope. Charlene cooks in the café. My mom and Mike own a motel that has a café in it. Charlene was already there before we came."

John nodded, finishing his cookie, and extended his hand. "My name is John. What's yours?"

The boy pushed his shaggy, wet hair aside from his deep brown eyes and shook hands. "Everybody calls me Scooter, except sometimes when my mom is mad, then she calls me Henry. That was my grand-father's name. I was named after him. I think Henry sounds dorky, don't you? Anyway, I never met my grandfather, so why should I have to be named after him? If any of the kids in school heard me called that . . ." He shuddered at the thought. "So you can just call me Scooter too, okay?"

John smiled, amazed at how long the boy could talk on one breath. His freckled cheeks and intelligent eyes were so full of life and fun that John shuddered at the memory of the lifeless face. "Hey pal, what were you doing out there on that raft? Especially on a river like this one?"

Scooter frowned, and his voice got low. "You're not going to tell my mom, are you? I mean, she knows I have a raft . . . had a raft. She don't like me doing it alone. Mike keeps saying he'll come down here and help me with it." Scooter shrugged. "But he don't."

Then, before John answered, the rain stopped as suddenly as it began. The air was washed clean, redolent with the natural perfume of clean earth and vegetation. John sucked his lungs full of the delicious air as he stood gingerly on his bruised leg. He let the air out slowly, savoring the joy of being alive.

John ran his hands over their shirts. "These are almost dry. Guess we can go now. Thanks for the hospitality." He put his shirt on. "Nice place you've got here. Oh, and if *you* talk to your mom about the raft, I won't have to."

Scooter tilted his head at John, looking him over as they emerged from the hut. "Okay, I'll tell her." Sighing, he added, "I guess I owe you big. Whatcha doin' here?"

John stretched and yawned. "I'm looking for work. What've you got?" he asked good-humoredly.

Scooter smiled, then rubbed his chin like a man three times his age. "Not me; Mike. He needs somebody now. At least that's what I heard my mom telling him this morning. I think they forget this is summer and I'm not in school. They don't usually talk business if they think I can hear. I heard them arguing about Mike's leg again. He broke it last week."

"Ouch." John rubbed his own leg, remembering a fall from a tree long ago, and the close call with the snag that morning. "How's Mike doing?"

"Not so good. He keeps bumping into things with it, and it hurts him. He can't get up the stairs with the crutches very easy. He slipped and slid down yesterday when he was goin' upstairs to fix something. My mom got real mad at him and said he shouldn't be tryin' to do all that stuff by himself. Mike yelled back that he wasn't made of money." Scooter's voice caught in his throat. "I *hate* it when they yell at each other."

John looked away out over the river, giving the boy a moment of privacy to compose himself. Scooter's eyes watered, and his breath came in spurts. It seemed to John that there must have been some bad times in the little fellow's past. John gave his own sigh, one of resignation that even precious young hearts often had to struggle with heavy burdens here on earth. Not by God's will, of course, John knew that, but through God's gift of agency to His children. *And oh, how we abuse it,* thought John, *to our sorrow and the sorrow of those around us!*

As they walked along the river path, John and Scooter looked north toward the east side of the Mississippi River where the little town of Hampton Corner, population 604, resided. Along the north side of the town was Hampton Creek, a tributary that ran into the Mississippi. Even Hampton Creek had its own small flood walls, though they seemed tiny compared to the levees lining the Mississippi. Hampton Corner sat right in the corner between the two waterways where the creek flowed into the Mississippi. Out of sight from John and Scooter, a bridge crossed the creek going north to the Tillman River Valley, a lush spread of acreage covered with prosperous farms. Some people called it the richest river-bottom farmland in the world. And both the farmers and the townsfolk were supposedly protected by the huge earthen levees.

John shook his head at the burgeoning Mississippi. "Don't like the look of that river. I surely don't."

Scooter brightened, relieved to have the earlier subject forgotten. "Yup. That's what everybody's saying. There's gonna be a flood some-where down here."

John surveyed the landscape, his eyes seeing beyond the present. "Yup, going to be," he agreed absently. His mind formed a picture, clear around the edges, but fuzzy in the center. He saw the flood, saw the struggles that all nearby would face. It would be a bad flood. That much was certain. Only the details were unknown.

Scooter put his hands on his hips and rocked back on his heels like he had seen some of the old farmers do. "Maybe *nothin'* will stop the river," he said seriously. "Mr. Franklin said the levee's leaking and maybe we ought to just pack it all up and let the river take what it wants."

John looked down at the boy. "The levee may be leaking, but it's not gone. We don't have to pack up and run, not yet. We at least have to try to make some kind of stand. You know what they say, 'God helps those who help themselves.' We have to *try*, Scooter."

Scooter peered up at John. "Won't the flooding—if it comes—won't it just wash everything away anyway?"

John put his arm around Scooter's shoulder. "It might. But that doesn't mean we shouldn't do what we can to stand up to it if there's a way to. We can't give up without a fight if there's a chance we can win. God didn't put us on this earth to fail. And He'll help us if we do all we can do first. So, if that flood comes, we'll just see what we can do with a whole lot of sandbags, hard work, and prayer."

Scooter looked into John's warm eyes and nodded in agreement.

John smiled at the earnest young boy. "Now, how about that job you offered?"

Scooter felt safe with John, a feeling he hadn't known much of in his short life. All he knew was that he liked him. He liked him a lot.

Scooter pointed up the path. "That way, into town."

* * *

Eight miles away in Ruma, the county seat of Randolph County, Undersheriff Raymond Floyde parked his patrol car in his assigned spot at the county sheriff's office and jail complex.

As he entered the building, the elderly secretary eyed him warily before continuing to type a report. She had worked there through more than one elected sheriff and countless deputies. As far as she was concerned, the *real* power in the county sheriff's office sat behind her desk.

Ray lifted his hand in acknowledgment, walking past her and down the hallway toward the sheriff's office just as her phone rang.

"Sheriff's office . . . What? I can't get that to you right now," protested the old woman. "No, I can't. What? I don't care what the county commissioners want, it's not my job. I told you that yesterday. I'll—"

Ray smiled. It was nice to have the old dragon distracted for a moment, to hear someone else doing battle with her for a change.

Her angry voice drifted down the hallway after him as she argued with her caller. "Alright, alright. That much I'll do. But it will take me a while." The secretary slammed the phone down, glared into the hallway after Ray, then went into the file room. The sound of slamming file drawers reached his ears.

Ray stopped in front of the sheriff's open door, but that was as far as he would go. Inside, the sheriff was stretched back in his chair, one foot propped casually on the desk, phone held to his ear as he murmured an occasional, "Uh-huh." The sheriff's office was sacred territory, entered by invitation only. Other deputies in the past had made the mistake of ignoring the unwritten rule, and their heads had come close to rolling across the floor. It hadn't taken long for folks to catch on that being casual with *this* sheriff, in *his* office, was *not* the thing to do. Ray didn't have a problem with that. The boss was the boss; he could run his outfit any way he wanted to. Ray did his job, did it well, and left well enough alone. Leaning his slim, lanky form back up against the wall, Ray folded his arms and waited.

\* \* \*

Inside the kitchen of the Starbright Motel and Café, John struggled to clean a large cooking pot. Now and then he paused to grimace and shake the cramp out of his hand. Scooter had gotten him a meal in the café, claiming his mother wouldn't mind. Afterward, John had insisted on paying for it by working it off.

Charlene, the cook, had taken a real shine to John. Watching him from the corner of her eye, she fervently wished she were thirty years younger. No man so cute had come into Hampton Corner in a long time. So if he was going to work at the motel, it was all right with her.

Someone tapped John on the shoulder. He turned his head to see a small, attractive woman with long, brown hair and tired eyes. "Hi. I understand my son thinks I should hire you."

John smiled and wiped his hands on his pants before shaking her hand. "My name is John. Your son was kind enough to arrange a meal for me, and Charlene let me pay for it by working."

The woman looked him straight in the eyes, taking his measure. She nodded slightly, as if to herself, before continuing. "I'm Linda Torres. My husband, Mike, and I own this crazy place. I hear you want a job?"

Scooter appeared seemingly out of nowhere beside John. "Yeah Mom, he needs a job. And Mike needs someone to help him. That's what you said. I heard you." Scooter squeezed John's muscular arm. "He's strong, Mom. He could help Mike, easy. He swam all the way out into the middle of the river to get me."

Linda's eyes widened with shock. "What did you say?"

Scooter seemed to shrink. How had that slipped out? The river, his raft, John saving him. That was one story he for sure didn't want to tell his mother.

"I don't know that it was the *middle* of the river," temporized John. "Perhaps closer to the shore."

"Were you down there with your raft again?" Linda demanded of her son, grabbing his arms as if to reassure herself he was really there.

"Mom, it's okay. *I'm* okay. My raft, it . . . uh . . ."

"It what?"

"Well, it kind of fell apart on me. I was just going to stay right next to shore but then the rope came loose and I started to drift and the logs came apart . . . I didn't *mean* for it to happen. Gee, Mom, Mike doesn't ever come help me with it like he promised." Scooter shamefully ducked his head and dug his toe into the floor.

"I *told* you not to go down there." Linda's pretty face was flushed with anxiety, her eyebrows knit together over intense, frightened eyes.

Scooter hung his head even lower. "I know, Mom. I didn't think anything bad would happen, honest. I'm sorry."

Linda paused as if to gather herself, took a deep breath, relaxed her shoulders, and smiled warmly at her only child. Wiping away a tear from her eye, she reached out and drew him close. The love she had for Scooter ran very deep. The two of them had been through a lot together. " I know you didn't mean to, buddy. I know. But I would die if I lost you, honey." Holding him tightly helped her to stop trembling, helped her to know Scooter was safe and right there with her. Her thoughts were racing, and she realized what might have happened if this man had not come along.

"Mom . . . Mom! You're gonna squish me!" came her son's muffled voice. Laughing shakily, she released her boy, ruffling his hair as she smiled thinly at John and quickly brushed at her eyes with the back of her hand. "Thank you. I think maybe you did a lot more than either of you are saying. I'm deeply in your debt."

John smiled and looked down into her deep, brown eyes. "It's okay. You're very welcome. He's a great kid you know." Changing the subject, John pointed at the pot in the dishwater. "So, how about a job?"

Linda nodded. "Okay, Scooter says you're our man. And Scooter tends to be a pretty good judge of character. I'd say we pretty well owe you that much anyway. We can't pay a whole lot, you know, but you *do* get room and board . . ." Her face clouded as she thought of Mike. Frowning, she turned and started for the door. "Now I better go break the good news to our resident grump."

\* \* \*

Linda was climbing the stairs to the second floor of the motel when she doubled over in sudden pain. For a moment, she couldn't even get her breath. She grasped the handrail tightly, her knuckles whitened, and she slid slowly down the wall to rest on the stairs. Sweat broke out on her forehead as she tried not to breathe any more than she had to. The courtyard swam before her eyes. After a moment that seemed to last eternities, the deep, burning pain eased a bit, and then was gone as fast as it had come, leaving Linda limp and shuddering.

When she could move again, she wiped her arm across her clammy forehead and pulled herself back up, then slowly continued upward, trying to ignore the telltale trembling in her legs.

Once inside their personal suite, she lay for a time on her bed, terrorizing herself with what the pain might mean. However, staying busy with life and the day-to-day demands had to be better than laying there, thinking about the innumerable possibilities. She carefully got up and went to her closet. Organizing her closet had always been thera-peutic for Linda. Mike teased her that he could always tell when she was upset about something by how many times she reorganized her closet. She shrugged it off, deciding that even if it were true, it didn't change the fact that it soothed her. Besides, nobody was ever kept out of heaven for having a closet too neatly organized! "Beats drinking!" she muttered out loud, then smiled to herself at the logic.

Linda straightened a box on the top shelf, and a photo slid off onto the floor. She picked it up and smiled as she saw what it was. She remembered that day at the beach by Lake Michigan. There they were, she and Mike. She dazzled the camera with her smile, while Mike draped a proprietary arm around her waist, pulling her close with a look of adoration in his eyes. A happy Scooter played busily at their feet in the sand. That had been *such* a good day.

Then Linda frowned.

When would Mike get tired of her and leave her? She was convinced that someday he would. Nothing in her life, other than Scooter, had ever worked out for very long. No one had ever been there for her. Her father had died when she was young, and her mother, so overwhelmed with the loss, shut herself up in her own world, leaving Linda to struggle alone. Her mother died shortly after

Linda's graduation from high school. The coroner had said it was a heart attack. Linda knew it was a broken heart.

Then there had been Linda's brief, violent marriage to a man ten years her senior. A man she met when she was struggling to survive on her own at age nineteen. A man who had promised to take care of her if she would share his bed and his life. But the initial joy in her newfound security was quickly crushed by the reality of his possessiveness and his need to control. She remembered all too well the days in the hospital when Scooter had been born, how the doctors fought to save her life. She had listlessly drifted, wishing to die, until a wise nurse had placed her newborn son into her arms and awakened in Linda a fierce determination to protect this little spark of life. It had been a long struggle; the bitter divorce, her husband's abandonment, the threats he made against her life, even against Scooter's life. She moved far away from all she had ever known to start completely over; no one to depend on, to ask for help or comfort. All alone, just her and Scooter. And she had done it. But she had come away believing there never would be anyone who would love and protect her forever as she loved and protected Scooter.

Even when Mike had miraculously come into her life, there was always the nagging fear, the deep belief that he would leave her too. And it haunted her deep in her soul, throwing a shadow of fear and caution into every bright moment they shared. When would Mike tell her he'd had enough of being a husband and father? Enough of taking care of this run-down motel? Or worse, far worse, maybe he wouldn't tell her. Maybe he'd just not be there someday.

Her fear of Mike's leaving was part of the reason she had changed her mind about having another child. It had seemed like a good idea at first. So many times Mike had talked of how much he wanted his own child. Not that he didn't love Scooter—he did; but he *needed* to have a child of his own blood, a babe he could love and cherish from birth onward. No matter what the doctors had told her when Scooter was born, a baby was worth it if it meant Mike would keep loving her. This would be *his* baby, *their* baby, and would tie Mike to her forever. And the first weeks of her pregnancy had been just fine.

Then the pain had started, even worse than when she had carried Scooter.

Linda's solution was not to tell anyone. After all, she knew what was wrong, so what was the point? Besides, she had never told Mike about what had happened in her pregnancy with Scooter, never told him the risk she might be taking. She was afraid if she had, he would have refused to give her this baby. And now she was afraid to tell him for fear he'd be angry at her for covering it up. Also they had no insurance, and no way to pay for any doctor visits, trips to the hospital for special care, special doctors, or for the abortion the doctor would surely recommend. No *way* was she going to lose this baby. This meant too much to her, to them both.

So each time the pain hit, each time she felt as if her insides would tear apart, and she really needed Mike to hold her and say everything would be all right, she stuffed it. And each time it happened she felt more.

Talking to God helped.

It had occurred to her that she could write Mike a letter, tell him everything. And then he could write back to her. That way each of them would have the time to deal with their feelings. But Linda had kept her letter; it remained hidden at the bottom of her "important papers" drawer in the motel office.

Every day Mike asked questions. Some of them were only with his eyes, but she could feel them. He could tell something was wrong, and he was afraid.

At first she thought he was worried about the motel, but when she asked about his worries he always made up something silly. She wished she could talk to him, get at the root of things, even if it were because . . .

Oh, how she ached to reassure her hero, the one she had given her whole heart to, the one she would give her life for, the best man she had ever known. But that meant telling Mike the truth about herself, that she might lose the baby. He would worry and blame himself. It was such an unbearable mess.

Linda squeezed her eyes shut as tight as she could. These painful thoughts and worries led her back into her past, to flashbacks of ugly, painful memories of her life before Mike. Those times from her first marriage, the days filled with accusations and threats. And more than a few beatings. Sometimes when she and Mike argued, she forgot it was her beloved Mike she was with, and slipped back to the bad times, screaming at him to leave her alone, to stop treating her like a child, to not touch her. Then it would be days before she could forgive herself, feeling worthless and hopeless and full of a terrible, heart-wrenching guilt.

She took long walks by the river, trying to work things out. Most of the time she hardly noticed where her feet took her. When she returned, she never had a good answer for her strange behavior. She would mumble an apology, frowning, too ashamed to even look Mike in the eyes. She knew sometimes he thought she was still angry with him, when in fact, she was still angry with herself.

Mike worried even more then, wondering if Linda was getting tired of him. Confused, unhappy, and unsure of what to do to make things better, Linda held tight to the thought that when the baby came it would all come right. When the baby came . . .

# chapter 2

Raymond was still waiting patiently. Sheriff George "Pete" Picou finally finished the phone call and spun around in his swivel chair, his feet hitting the floor with a bang. Behind him on the wall was a dated photo of himself, his eyes barely visible under the shadow of his hat. He was leaning up against his old John Deere tractor in worn-out jeans and a plaid shirt. He had been a farmer for many years, and he still wore the deep tan on his face and arms. But that was all before— before deciding he was the one to change the way things ran around Randolph County, instead of just living his life as a quiet bachelor with a large farm to run.

And now there was still no ring on his left hand, and no wife wondering when he was coming home. "I just never got around to it," was what Pete always said when he was asked, as he inevitably was.

"Come on in, Ray. Sorry I'm late for the meeting . . . the call . . ." he waved his hand at the phone. Pete settled more comfortably into his prized high-back swivel chair. The vintage leather cushions made a soft swishing sound, and the undercarriage creaked as he leaned back.

As Raymond entered Pete's "sacred ground," he glanced over at the plaques on the wall. There was one from the Lions, one from the Grange, another from the Shriners, the VFW, and even the Elks. At fifty-four years old, he was the most senior elected official in the county and very popular. Everyone knew that the prematurely white-haired man was *the* power in local politics. Raymond himself said that the sheriff was the one you went to when you needed things done.

"Meetings with the county commissioners always take forever," complained Pete, "and talking to them on the phone is just as bad.

You'd think they'd say it all in the meetings, but they don't. There's always 'just one more thing.'" He snorted in disgust. The toothpick in his mouth disintegrated into smaller and smaller slivers with each angry gnash of his teeth. He yanked it out of his mouth and threw the pieces into the trash barrel next to his desk. "What a bunch of windbags. There's enough hot air in that group to power the Goodyear Blimp."

Raymond blinked, but said nothing. He agreed, but there was no point in getting into it. You could rant all day about that crew and never get anything else done. It was life, that's all.

Pete shook his head, not in the least deterred by Raymond's silence. "At least people in Randolph county trust *me*. You know why? Because they know they'll get an honest response and prompt action. And I know how to work with the other officials to get the needed things done. I don't waste my time with 'fancy dancin'!'"

Raymond smiled a little. Other elected officials knew the sheriff as the guy never to cross. More than once he had gone head to head with the whole county commission, and won. Not an easy feat in any county, anywhere. Pretty miraculous actually.

Pete rubbed his temple. One of his migraine headaches was beginning, and a sharp pain stabbed his left eye. "What's the report on the levees?"

Deliberately, Raymond began his report. "From what *I* can see they look strong. I talked to Herman Mombow, and he said the Levee District has begun stockpiling sandbags. But their call for volunteers isn't going too well. Seems there's a rumor going around that it's hopeless and everyone might as well pack up and let the water do what it wants. And then there's the other bunch who figure they'll just pray for a miracle, no muscle needed."

Pete rubbed the pain in his temple and squinted at Raymond. Maybe talking to Undersheriff Floyde was part of the problem. He was a good man; solid, responsible, dependable, but somehow, not someone you wanted for a friend. The deputy was quiet, detached, even taciturn. Not that Pete was exactly much of a talker himself. But there was something real different about Ray, like his name for example: he didn't like his name shortened. If you asked him, he'd tell you he preferred to be called Raymond, not Ray, even though everyone called him Ray. It seemed a little *unnatural,* somehow. Pete just couldn't get past that.

Pete shifted in his chair, bringing his attention back to Ray's report. As Ray talked, Pete could well imagine Herman Mombow, the president of the Levee District, in yet another analysis group meeting, urging that all was okay . . . That guy could study things to death, but what they needed was *action.*

"Idiots," he said to Raymond. "Maybe they're expecting Charlton Heston to show up here and part the sea like he did in *The Ten Commandments.*" Leaning forward on his desk he picked up a fax message, glanced at it, and said, "This came in just this morning. The Illinois Emergency Preparedness Department thinks the area north of St. Louis will get hit the hardest."

Raymond envisioned that area of the state and the flood waters bunching up as they hit St. Louis, the back flowing upstream, and the resulting back flooding that would inevitably occur. The vision was frightening.

"They figure they'll be able to deflect a lot of the water and don't seem to think we'll get all that much here," continued Pete. He tossed the paper to one side of his desk. He flipped what was left of his latest toothpick across the room into a trash basket. After popping another into his mouth, he continued, "They're wrong. Flood's coming. It doesn't take a genius to see that. And we don't need some intellectual types to tell us how to take care of things."

Pushing back from his desk and yawning widely, Pete shook his head in frustration. He hadn't slept much the past few weeks. Instead he found himself lying awake nights, thinking. He had already talked to some other sheriffs he knew northward along the river, all the way up into Minnesota. No matter what the "experts" thought, he was sure it was no longer a matter of if, but *when* the flood was coming south.

Pete settled back in his chair again. "So, Ray, what do *you* think? Is all this worry and effort going to be for nothing? Reports up north say you can't sandbag high enough to stop it."

Pete sighed, and before Ray could answer, words came pouring out of his mouth even before he knew he was going to say them. "I'm tired. I'm starting to feel too old and too tired for all this. This job just feels heavier every day."

An awkward silence fell between the two men. Raymond was stunned. The sheriff had never confided in him before . . . it just wasn't his style. Pete was stunned too. He and Raymond had worked together for years, but their interactions never went beyond the professional before now. What on earth had come over him? Maybe he really *was* losing it. Embarrassed, Pete busied himself by scribbling a note on a piece of paper, pretending he hadn't just shared something personal.

Raymond took the cue and turned to look at the county map on the wall, reviewing the twenty-five miles of Randolph County riverbank area. He'd been thinking a lot about the flooding, but had decided to keep his thoughts to himself unless Pete wanted to know. Now, it seemed, maybe Pete wanted to know. He drew a line on the chalkboard that hung in Pete's office. "Here's the Mississippi. And here," he marked another line, "is Hampton Creek. Right here in the corner, right where they come together, is the town. I think our problem is going to happen not on the Mississippi part, but on the Hampton."

Pete nodded, not really paying attention to what Raymond was telling him. His migraine was getting worse. The spots were starting before his eyes, and he was getting sick to his stomach.

"I keep wondering," continued Raymond, "if the worst trouble will come from the levee up north at Valmeyer. The whole levee system from Valmeyer to Hampton is leaking, but the trouble spot might be there."

"Valmeyer is Monroe County's problem," said Pete. It felt like there were hot pins in his eye.

Raymond nodded. "Right. But if *that* river levee goes down, if *it* buckles, that will send water down the valley at us. If the water goes far enough, and runs into the small flood walls on Hampton Creek, I think there might be real trouble, and then it'll be *our* problem."

Valmeyer was the little town that lay due north of Hampton Corner in the long, narrow river-bottom area called the Tillman River Valley. Valmeyer and Hampton Corner anchored opposite ends of the area that lay east between the river and rising hills. And Hampton Corner was Raymond's home.

Pete's phone rang. He sat up, grabbed it, and growled, "What?"

Raymond set the chalk down on the board rail, dusting his hands on his pants.

"Yeah, okay. Give me ten minutes." Pete hung up abruptly. "Commissioners thought of something else they just got to talk to me about. But you keep right on thinking, Ray, and let me know if things get worse. If they do, we're going to need to really jump."

Clearly, Raymond was being dismissed. He looked at Pete for a moment, wondering if anything he said had gotten through to the sheriff, then shrugged and turned on his heel to walk out the door.

After he could no longer hear Ray's footsteps echoing down the hallway, Pete got up to look out the window. From his office he had a clear view of the town of Rama, but in his mind he could see even beyond that, through the trees behind the courthouse to where the little town of Hampton Corner lay nestled beside the Mississippi. Pete had lived his whole life in southern Illinois, growing up on a farm in the Tillman River Valley; he would have still been there too if he hadn't been sheriff for the last twenty years. He was as much a part of the land as the trees and hills. Sometimes he felt like the only thing more deeply rooted around here was the river.

Briefly he allowed his mind to wander through Hampton Corner, coming to stand beside the park statue of Colonel Henry Hampton. Off to the left, across the parking lot next to the grocery store, would be the old Hudson home. It was boarded up now, but he could remember when people lived in it. Shoot, that house had been old when he was a kid. Even then, as now, people had built their homes and lived beside the river. Those people wouldn't have just picked up and run, no matter how high the water got. More than one older structure in the area had water marks on their lower levels where floods had come and gone.

From the Hudson house Pete would also be able to see the Starbright Motel, now owned by that young woman and her Mexican husband. Pete had stopped by there once to visit just after they bought the place, to get a piece of Charlene's famous pie, and to get to know the young couple. They seemed like good, hardworking people. He'd been impressed with how the man had looked him straight in the eyes, no flinching, no attitude. And his young wife was a bright one, no doubt about it. If anyone could make a go of that place, those two probably could. Right now though, that motel was sitting in a bad spot. A *real* bad spot.

The Starbright Motel had been built some twenty-five years ago on land reclaimed from the river, right where the Mississippi and Hampton met. Some fast-talking real estate man or developer had managed to sell that dumb idea to some poor idiot. Twenty-five years ago there hadn't been a major flood in the area since the levees had been built. That didn't mean there never *would* be another one. Pete shook his head in disgust.

After contemplating all the possibilities for disaster for several more minutes, he rubbed his temples. "Old Man River, I know you're coming. I can feel you. I just hope it won't be as bad as I think it's going to be."

* * *

Mike Torres poked at the closet wall next to him with one of his crutches. "I didn't ask for any help around here. This is *our* motel." His face was tight, his brows furrowed in frustration. As always, his shirt sleeves were rolled up and his collar loosened. But his hair was neatly combed, and he kept his face closely shaved, except for a thin mustache. Having to wear jeans slit up the side for his cast bothered him. Since leaving Mexico he had vowed to always dress his best—present himself well. "Hey, are you listening to me?" he called again. The only answer was the sound of boxes being moved around. Once more, Linda was organizing their closet. Linda had been doing this more and more lately. It scared him because it seemed like she did it to avoid him; or to avoid his questions at least . . . but then she avoided his eyes sometimes too. What was eating at her?

Mike had learned it was a habit—this organizing—that went all the way back to her childhood. Mike hoped that's all it was now. He would go crazy if it were something else, if she were trying to get away from him somehow. He would go crazy if she ever left him, if he ever failed her.

He remembered his first attempt to make this place hers—to prove to her that he was serious about her dreams. Mike had knocked out a wall between two of the motel suites to make their living area larger. Part of what he had reconstructed was a huge walk-in closet. She kept both parts, hers and Mike's, very well organized. Drawers were sorted from top to bottom. The carpeted floor was always kept vacuumed. And an air freshener hung from one of the bars. You could *live* in Linda's closet. How could anybody be that compulsive? Thank goodness she wasn't that way with everything . . . just the closet. It made living with her a whole lot easier.

"I know you didn't ask for any help," she answered, finally stepping out from among the closet organizer racks she had installed a few months ago. "But we did talk about doing something different so you wouldn't be so tempted to overdo it while your leg is healing. Honestly Mike, I know that if you were in top shape it wouldn't even be a question; you are more than capable of handling it all yourself . . ." She paused as she took something out of a drawer, refolded it, and placed it into another drawer.

"I didn't know that meant you were going to hire someone."

"It's only part-time. The man said that's all he wanted. Besides, it's not just to help you out; it's a chance for us to help someone *else* out. This guy seems kind of down on his luck and could really use a job for a while. And I know you have such a good heart, you wouldn't really mind, just for a little while," she wheedled. That was when she spotted it. Earlier that day morning sickness had pulled her into the bathroom. She had been coming out and wiping her face with a towel after throwing up when Mike unexpectedly entered their suite. Startled, she tossed the towel into the back of the closet. Now, from where she was standing, she could see it behind Mike. Somehow she had to inconspicuously retrieve it. Now was definitely not the time to tell him about their baby.

"Um, Mike? Will you look out by the bed and see if my robe is there?"

Mike was confused. "What? You always put your robe away. You're the neatest per—"

She pointed, and gently nudged him toward the bed. When he had gone only two steps, she lunged for the towel, and put it behind her back.

Looking on the floor beside the bed, Mike said, "I don't see it."

She looked up at her robe, hanging where she always put it during the day. "Silly me, here it is. You were right after all."

Mike gave her a strange look. Linda was stuffing something into a drawer. The woman who never failed to brush her teeth and fix her hair before kissing him awake each morning had sure been acting different lately. What was bothering her?

Mike hobbled back into the closet and poked again at the wall with his crutch, the rubber tip making a satisfying thump. "So, who is this guy?"

"Who?"

"The guy you hired."

"Oh, him. Scooter met him down by the river and brought him home."

"Oh, great! Now we're hiring river bums."

Linda knew her man well. Mike blustered at times, but there wasn't any meanness in him. She could always wait patiently for him to calm down, as he always did. He had a big heart for those he considered sincerely down and out. His own life had been hard enough to teach him compassion, the quality she had been most drawn to when they first met.

When Mike's fiery temper did flare, it was brief, and without malice. She never feared his words or his fists. And when he did lose his temper and yell at her, no one was sweeter about making it up to her. How different he was from her first husband.

Linda shook herself out of her musings, coming back to the present and the current problem.

She touched Mike's arm. "Sweetheart, he's not a bum. He's . . . he's different. I can't explain it, but I'd trust Scooter with this guy. Doesn't that say something?"

Mike reluctantly nodded. Linda trusted Scooter with almost no one. "Okay, okay. But, what am I supposed to do now, go fishing?"

"Hey, you're the all-important boss man!" Linda punched him playfully on the arm. "You tell him what to do. John can be your legs. Big-time business man, just like the big boys." Suddenly soft and serious, Linda leaned gently up against Mike and kissed his chin. "Besides, we can't have you hurting yourself again, or your leg will never heal."

Mike never could stay upset when Linda talked so low and gentle. The tough street kid from Mexico City just melted when he was with her. She had even convinced him to join her "Mormon Church," though he never felt all that welcome there. For that matter, he never felt all that sure of himself anywhere here in this new life, except with Linda. But Linda said she was sure about the Church, and he believed her when she told him she knew it was true. He'd just have to keep working on believing for himself.

Pulling gently out of Mike's arms into a more upright position, Linda became businesslike. "Okay, where's your list?"

Mike smiled at the running joke between them about his never-ending list of things to do around the motel. He fished it out of his back pocket. "It's just a little one today," he kidded.

Linda smiled as she scanned the long list. "How about I go rescue John from Charlene and send him to the office so you can get him started."

Mike envisioned gruff old Charlene running this John guy ragged. When Charlene got going about what needed to be done and how it needed to be done, Mike sometimes had a hard time remembering who really was the boss!

Catching his thought by the look on his face, Linda chuckled. "It's not like that. John has charmed her. She thinks he's wonderful. Charlene's acting like she's a kid again. Heck, I didn't realize she even knew *how* to flirt! You really ought to see this, it's pretty amazing."

Mike's eyes widened. "Charlene *flirting?* This guy I have to meet."

As Mike left, Linda reflected on the lucky chance that had brought them together. On an early spring day over four years ago, she had been at a playground with her young son enjoying the fresh spring air and warm sunshine. Suddenly there came shouts across the playground and the shrill voice of a frightened child. Linda stood up quickly and turned toward the direction of the noise. Several larger boys were grouped around a smaller child, perhaps no more than eight or nine years old. They were yelling at him, grabbing and shoving him, and the little one was in tears, trying desperately to pull away.

Instinctively Linda reacted. "Scooter, stay here! I'll be right back!" And she ran toward the boys, realizing somewhat belatedly that the boys were as tall as she was and perhaps fifteen or sixteen years old. "Too late to back out now, lady," she muttered to herself and kept running. Before she reached them though, a man came charging out of nowhere. Yelling in Spanish what Linda presumed were swear words, he certainly sounded angry enough. Unhesitatingly he dove in between the boys, and tucking the younger boy into him with one arm, continued his barrage of words. His language may not have been understandable, but his intent was unmistakable. He was slim and not too tall, standing only an inch or two taller than the tallest boy, but what he lacked in size he made up for in intensity.

The older boys hesitated, looked at each other, and with one last curse, they ran.

Gasping for breath, Linda dashed to the man who still had the small boy grasped tightly in his arms. Before she could say a word, the man dropped to his knees before the terrified child.

"Are you okay, little one? Did they hurt you?" he asked, gently looking the child over, brushing grass and dirt off his pants. "Why were they bothering you, muchacho?"

The boy began crying. "They wanted the money my mom gave me to go to the store. They followed me and took it. They wanted me to get more money for them. They said they'd k-kill me!"

The man cursed softly under his breath, then hugged the child. "C'mon, amigo. No one will hurt you. Let's go find your mother and a policeman."

Linda had introduced herself to the man, then gathered up Scooter and gone along to take the child home and to talk to the police. She had never forgotten the incident, and the kind of caring it took for a man, obviously not born in this country, to put himself out over another's troubles. That was Mike—and it was only a matter of time before they found they needed each other. *Kindred spirits. Soul mates.* Words Linda had thought were just silly expressions in some songwriter's repertoire. Until Mike.

As Mike unfolded his story to her during their long, sweet courtship, she was even more drawn to his quiet strength and courage. He had never known his father. And his mother, a prostitute in Mexico City, died when he was five. He was left to fend for himself on the streets and had survived by learning young who he could trust. Begging for handouts, he was part of a gang—the only family he had ever known—who fought for each other and *with* each other. Hurt in a street fight when he was fifteen, Mike was taken by some visiting American Peace Corps workers to a local hospital. It was those same workers who made sure Mike was treated by the annoyed doctors,

doctors who assured them the street rat wasn't worth the trouble. The Americans paid Mike's bills, and when he was released, took him back to their camp outside a small village not too far from the Texas border. In the next six months, they taught Mike to read and write real English, not just the street pidgin he had learned to use for begging. Deeply impressed with his bright mind and willing heart, the workers made Mike into a sort of camp mascot. Unbeknownst to Mike, word about him spread through the group of Americans he worked with, and beyond. After a year of working as an unofficial member of the Peace Corps, Mike was approached by a senior official and offered the chance of a lifetime—the opportunity to go to the States and get an education. A wealthy benefactor had been contacted by a friend in the corps and had arranged to help Mike. He was stunned beyond words. Finally, he stuttered out a heartfelt blessing on all those who God had sent to help him. At just seventeen years of age, Mike Torres was offered a new lease on life. It was like a fairy tale, a dream come to life.

The next four years of Mike's life passed quickly in a blur of hard work and happiness. Mike repaid his benefactors by working hard and "keeping his nose clean." He completed a bachelor's degree in business from a Dallas, Texas, community college, earning scholastic scholarships after his first year. Upon graduation, he was given a $3,000 check from his friends and benefactors and their best wishes for his future. It had seemed like so much then, and still did even now. In the past twelve years Mike had worked hard to justify all that had been given him; he had saved hard too, working first as store manager in a convenience store, then moving to another state where he worked as an assistant manager for a large grocery store chain in a northern city far away from Mexico and his past. There he had finally won full citizenship, and there he had met Linda. Mike still woke up nights in a sweat, thinking it was all a dream, reaching out to hold Linda in his arms to reassure himself this was truly his life here—so much goodness out of so much darkness. He repaid those who had given him this chance by working as hard as he could, vowing he would take care of his family, his wife, and when he could, others.

Knowing all about Mike's strength, quiet courage, and desire to do and be good, had sealed her heart to his. She was humbled to think he had chosen to be with her—to raise another man's child as his own, to love another man's cast-off, as she was. She knew now that Mike was too good for her. How could she not love him? And she trembled to think of the day when he, too, might wake up and realize that he was too good for her and leave. It was this joy from her love for Mike, it was this terror from what she believed was inevitable, that Linda Torres lived with day by day.

# chapter 3

It was late afternoon that summer day at the MacFarland farm, six miles north of Hampton Creek. Upstairs in the old farmhouse, Sandy MacFarland was planning to head out for Hampton Corner. That is, as soon as she could get herself into some town clothes. Her pants, however, were not cooperating. Earlier Sandy's daughter, Natalie, had produced another fine midday meal. And that was precisely the problem. Sandy loved to eat—and it showed in the excess inches on her waist and hips.

"C'mon, give me a break," Sandy pled with her jeans, lying back on the bed, rocking from side to side as she struggled to pull the fabric close enough to get the zipper up. "Darn pants! I must've run them through the wash cycle with hot water or something." Pride wouldn't let her admit her figure was expanding again. Sandy firmly believed she could put on weight just by looking at food, a trait she was sure she had inherited from her mother. The scale was her enemy, first lulling her into a sense of false security as her weight stabilized, then, without warning, it would show that her weight had begun to sneak up on her. *It's really not fair. I don't eat any more than anyone else, and a whole lot less than others I could name!*

Just the same, Sandy was an attractive woman, although perhaps not in the classical sense. She was more along the lines of what some kindly referred to as "statuesque." She often consoled herself by reciting Marilyn Monroe's lusciously rounded measurements at the time she starred in *Some Like It Hot,* because in that sense Sandy wasn't too far off the mark set by that legendary beauty. It was a point of pride to her to not go above a certain size, no matter what. At the moment she was pushing the upper reaches of that, and she was well aware she'd have to change things pretty darn quick or end up in a house dress.

With a superhuman tug, she managed to get the zipper closed. Rolling off the bed, she paused for a moment on her knees, trying to breathe; then rising carefully, she walked stiffly and uncomfortably to the bathroom, muttering under her breath. "They'll stretch out. They *will* stretch out," she repeated like a mantra. The pants might stretch some, but it would take a while. "Ooohh, my!" she moaned softly, bending her knees in an effort to stretch the material more quickly. She glanced over her shoulder in the mirror at her rear view. The pants were obviously tight, but her shirttails would hide any indecencies. She didn't want to look improper for heaven's sake!

She ran a brush quickly through her shoulder-length, strawberry blonde hair, stopping to note the strands of white that were becoming more and more evident. She then took a moment to inspect her face. At forty-seven, she was three years older than her second husband, Jeff. They had been married for sixteen years, and Sandy had become a true farm wife. Well, almost. It hadn't been easy, that was for sure. After growing up in Los Angeles, she still found it hard to accept "real" country ways sometimes. She was sure the early mornings and often late nights had contributed to those new lines on her face and the sprinkling of white in her hair. But life with Jeff had been good for the most part. He was a good man, and she loved him. Thinking over the years they had shared together, she grinned. It had been worth it.

Staring at her reflection in the mirror, Sandy frowned at the wrinkles by her eyes. Called "laugh lines" by the gracious, to her they were an enemy that resisted every ointment she could buy. Yet another sign of age. Where *did* the years go? Still, the eyes were pretty—deep green, with flecks of gold. They had character, and maybe their sparkle would keep people from noticing the lines.

She thought of her twin sister, Mandy. She had no lines on her face. Being married to a cosmetic surgeon had its perks. At least *my* face is *real*, Sandy consoled herself. She wondered briefly if she was vain. It was a sin to be vain. "Naw," she said out loud to her mirror, "Just like to be the best I can be. 'Do not go graceful into that dark night . . .'[1] or something like that!"

Dropping her brush in a cabinet drawer, she grabbed her purse from the dresser, and moved gingerly down the stairs, wondering where she had left her good shoes and if the pants were going to stretch enough so she could drive to town in them. Dirty dishes from her daughter's meal of pork chops, mashed potatoes with gravy, and white cake and ice cream were partially cleared off the big dining table. "Thanks for everything, sweetie," said Sandy, kissing her youngest child on the cheek as she passed by.

Natalie smiled lopsidedly while continuing to clear the table. The teenager thought to herself that if she had to do all this for another week she would go crazy.

"Mom?"

"Yeah, hon," answered Sandy from the mud room, an unheated enclosed porch off the kitchen where everyone kept their boots, coats, and hats, and where the large deep freezes were.

"Can I go with you?"

"What about the dishes . . ." Sandy stopped herself. She could tell by her daughter's tone of voice that this was no "lazy kid" request to get out of a job. Natalie more than carried her share around the farm. With one of her good shoes on, and the other foot bare, Sandy poked her head back into the kitchen. "Something the matter?"

Natalie plopped down in her father's high-backed chair at the head of the table, a look of utter hopelessness on her face. Sudden tears filled her eyes.

"Oh, baby. What is it?" Sandy crooned and walked over to hug her little one.

"I'm never going to be anyone. I'll never go anywhere. I'm always going to be cooking and washing dishes and cleaning and . . ." Natalie could hardly talk, her words just choking past her sobs. "I'll never be a real writer like Ray Bradbury. He writes such wonderful things. If I could only be like him. But everything I write is so . . . juvenile."

All of Sandy's hurry was pushed aside. She had needed her own share of hugs and comfort over her lifetime, and though nobody was tougher than Sandy when she had to be, she was the first to respond to others' pain with love. She had lived through her first husband's long and agonizing death to bone cancer, and the even longer, more painful months following his death when the only thing that seemed to keep her alive was the need to care for her little boy Robbie. Then she had survived Robbie's death in an accident only two years ago. She had wondered then if she were going to get through; some days she was certain she would go crazy. But she *had* gotten through, and pulled the rest of the family through with her. And when someone needed a gentle heart, a friendly ear, and hope, she was always there.

Pulling Natalie close under her chin she consoled her. "Baby, you won't be here forever. Your dad and I'll make sure you can go off to college. You're going to be the writer you were meant to be. I promise." After a moment she added, "Hey, I think you're right. Let's rinse and stack this mess together so you can come with me."

"But, I—"

"Nope! No argument. I'm the boss, remember? The dishes can wait. C'mon baby, you need a break. Everybody does sometimes. We'll catch it all up later."

Natalie wiped her eyes and brushed her blonde bangs back, hope cautiously lighting her face. "If Dad comes in and finds the kitchen like this he won't like it," she warned.

"Oh," Sandy blew a raspberry. "Men! They can leave their mess all over the place, but leave one dirty dish in the sink, and they start whining. You're going into town with me. The kitchen is *my* kingdom, not your father's." Sandy winked. "Besides, there's a surprise for him at the post office. That should sweeten him up." Snapping a kitchen towel at nothing in particular, Sandy started grabbing dishes off the table and marched to the sink whistling happily.

Natalie brightened. Today was her parent's wedding anniversary. At least tonight there would be some fun to break the monotony.

\* \* \*

Jeff MacFarland was grinding corn in the shed behind the main hog terminal when Sandy drove up to the shed door in the red pickup truck. She honked once, twice, and a third time, impatiently refusing to get out and dirty her only pair of good shoes. The hog smell that overwhelmed most people didn't even faze her anymore after so many years. Sometimes she wondered if her nose had been cauterized by the stink. Sandy honked again. Finally, Jeff came out of the building.

"Don't forget to pick up some more vials. Those five sows will be delivering any day now," he called out even before he got to the truck. He walked over and stuck his head through the open passenger-side window.

Sandy rolled her eyes. She had been in charge of immunizing the baby pigs for years, and knew more about that end of their 300-head hog business than Jeff did. But he still thought he had to remind her. Ignoring his comment, she nodded at Natalie. "I'm taking in some help. She needs a break, and I like her company."

"I suppose you'll want a raise too?" Jeff reached in to tickle his only daughter. "You're already the best paid cook and cleaner in the state."

Natalie crinkled up her nose. She loved her father dearly, even when that meant enduring his "farm life is the only life" lectures. To her he was far more than just another farmer with a tan line across his forehead and the perennial, green John Deere ball cap parked on his head. He was a tall man, lean and tough from years of hard physical labor. To his daughter he was a hero, like someone out of an old western story who battled with the land and elements to provide for his family. Her heart swelled with emotion for the second time today.

"Daddy, I . . ." The family writer's words failed her. Whenever things bottled up inside she could hardly speak. Where did all the tears come from? she wondered, surprised at herself.

Sandy reached over and grasped Natalie's shoulder. "We won't be long. You just remember where you hid my anniversary present. Because if I don't get one, then you don't either."

Jeff winked at Natalie and blew Sandy a kiss. "Ah, you'd still love me. Even if I never, ever gave you a present."

"I wouldn't push your luck too far on that one, buster," Sandy teased back. A fleeting thought about the last two years touched Sandy: Robbie's death, Jeff's depression, the never-ending struggle just to keep the farm and themselves going. They had shared so much together—deepening the bond between them past what she knew was possible. She smiled into his eyes as she shifted the truck into reverse and pulled carefully away. What they had went beyond the wrinkles and too-tight jeans.

As the truck left, Jeff waved and went back into the grinding shed. When he was sure there was enough corn to keep the machine going for a while, he headed over to check on his twin sons, Jason and

Jarod. They might be nineteen, but they still needed someone to keep them going on every little thing. Too bad they weren't more like Robbie had been. Now *there* was a person who would have grown up to be *someone*.

Thoughts of Robbie triggered the familiar twisting sensation in Jeff's gut. It was his fault Robbie was dead, his fault Sandy had lost her oldest son and first child. All over a little bit of money. Even though Sandy had never made him feel that way, Jeff knew it was so. That was the knowledge he would have to live with for the rest of his life. It haunted him, ate at his heart, made him feel old and helpless. *Too late now. Too late. I'm sorry Robbie, I'm so sorry . . .*

Jeff picked up a shovel one of the twins had carelessly left lying around, shook his head and sighed deeply. Back to the here and now. Weren't those guys ever going to grow up?

* * *

The old truck was always so noisy; usually riding in silence was easier than trying to make conversation over the noise. But this was a time for talking. Sandy weighed her words carefully. Natalie didn't need the "get-a-backbone" talk. That was one of Jeff's favorite lectures to the twins. What her daughter needed was a verbal hug, and starting too soon would just make Natalie's troubles worse.

As the truck moved steadily toward Hampton Creek and the bridge, they drove by Widow Poulson's place. The old woman had so many cats, even she didn't know how many there were. One of them, a tabby-colored fellow, was stalking a bird along the front hedge. Sandy smiled as the bird nonchalantly flew up into a nearby tree, leaving a frustrated cat swishing his tail furiously.

"You know," began Sandy, "I read the other day that hogs are passing broiler chickens as the number one agricultural commodity. If that keeps up, maybe someday we'll be rich after all!" Even as she said it, Sandy frowned at the stupidity of the topic.

Natalie was smart enough to receive straight talk. Smart enough to pull down A's, though lately she had been struggling some. Sandy cleared her throat as she struggled to think of how to start again.

Natalie saved her the trouble. "Mom, who am I?"

Looking sidelong at her attractive, intelligent daughter, Sandy thought of a million ways to answer. That was the kind of question it was easy to be light with, and wrong to do so. The kind you could precariously fall off the ledge into nothing with, and never get back to the important stuff. She considered it carefully before replying.

"Hmm. Kind of a tough question there, sweetie. You are so many wonderful things. You're my daughter. You are a sister, a promising young writer, a smart girl, a kind friend, a cute kid, and a good person, and that's only the *short* list. Who do *you* think you are?"

Natalie shrugged her shoulders heavily, eyes glued to the floorboards.

"You know we love you, don't you?"

Natalie nodded. "It's not that, Mom. It's just, well . . . sometimes I just wonder about what happens . . . after we die." She looked out the window beside her, then pulled something out of her shirt pocket. "This is a leaf from the tree that killed Robbie. I've been saving it." She touched it with love. "Mr. Brown said that some people believe the spirit of the deceased becomes part of the place they die in."

Sandy glanced quickly at the leaf encased in plastic. "Mr. Brown? Your science teacher told you that?"

Natalie nodded. "He helped me put plastic on it this year. I got an A on it."

Whenever Robbie's name was mentioned, conversation came to a stop among MacFarland family members. Now was no different. Sandy drove along silently until they were almost out onto the bridge. Sandy thought that maybe all that family silence hadn't been such a good idea. Not that she'd let it happen on purpose . . . it was just a habit they had all fallen into after Robbie's death—a way to avoid the pain and loss. It had been worse than when she had lost Adam to cancer. *And Lord knows that was painful enough. I thought I'd never get over it. I guess in some ways I haven't. Oh, Adam! I still miss you so much! My first love, my high school sweetheart, my handsome young husband.*

Adam was Robbie's father, and losing Robbie had been like losing Adam all over again. But at least with Adam's death she had known it was coming, had been able to prepare a bit for the inescapable. But Robbie hadn't been sick. He had been young, smart, strong, full of energy, life and promise. It was so *wrong* for him to die like that. *Guess that's why they call them "accidents,"* she thought wryly to herself.

Sighing at her thoughts, Sandy addressed her daughter's pain. "I miss him too, honey. I expect we always will, all of us. That's just part of the risk of truly loving someone."

"Do you think we stop existing when we die?" Natalie watched her mother's face intently, seeking answers to her pain and wondering if there *were* any answers.

"No way!" Sandy responded.

"How do you know?" Natalie persisted. "Marjorie Wilson says God is just something people made up so they don't have to take responsibility for themselves. Someone they can blame things on, or claim created some kind of 'miracle.' She says only weak, scared, stupid people pretend to believe in God. That strong, smart folks don't 'cause they can face life on their own."

Sandy mentally went over a few choice words regarding Marjorie Wilson's mother, the most vocal atheist in the county, but bit her tongue so as not to verbalize them. "That is what the Wilsons believe. Not us. Remember that movie? The one about the guy who gets killed, but hangs around to help his girlfriend be safe from some bad guys? Boy, that story really got to me. Remember how I cried and cried and embarrassed you half to death? But I believe that's kind of how it is. We *do* keep existing somehow, in some way; we don't just disappear into nothingness. *That* would make no sense! Sweetheart, I know it with all my heart. I can *feel* it with my whole soul. It's not just hogwash. It's the truth. You can count on it."

Shrugging noncommittally, Natalie put the leaf back in her pocket. "Sometimes I feel so bad about Robbie. It just kills me. He never got to go anywhere really. His life ended so young. That was *wrong*, Mom. If there really *is* a God, why did he let that happen to Robbie?"

Before Sandy could think of an answer, the truck bounced over a bump in the road, and the transmission slipped for a moment before catching again. Sandy had to struggle to get the old truck back under control. "You know, Natalie, when Robbie was a baby and Robbie's daddy was dying, I thought I was going to die too. I couldn't believe God would take him from Robbie and me. Robbie was *so little*. I struggled and struggled with that until I thought I'd go crazy. I prayed and cried until I thought my knees were gonna fall off and my eyeballs would shrivel into raisins! But finally a friend helped me see that this life is only temporary. The fact of the matter is, stuff happens. If God stepped in and rescued us from every bad thing, protected us from every hurt that came our way, stopped all unfairness from touching our lives, what kind of people would we turn out to be? I mean, if you chip away the eggshell from around the baby chick so he doesn't have to work so hard getting born, what happens? He dies. You know that, don't you? He *needs* the struggle to make him strong enough to face life. That's why we struggle. If God protected us from all that life brings, we would be weak and die, just like the baby chicks. God loves us enough to let us struggle, and He loves us enough to give us the strength to endure the pain. *Love* is real—the love we share with others. It's *that* love that I know will hold us all together forever. Someday we'll see everybody we love again, and be with them too. I know it." Sandy sat back a moment, stunned by her own verbosity, wondering if the words that had tumbled so freely from her heart had made any sense to her troubled young daughter. So many of the things she had said were thoughts she had never spoken to anyone before, but had kept hidden deep within, nursing them as hope and solace for her own wounded heart.

Silent, Natalie ran her hand along the truck dashboard, contemplating her mother's words. When she spoke, her eyes were dreamy, faraway. "I dreamed about Robbie last night. I could see him clear as day. Even the dimple in his cheek, ya' know? He was standing in my room, right next to my bed. He told me the floods were coming, and that the levee wouldn't hold. Then, he left. Mom, it looked just like him, it even *felt* like him, like he was really there." Natalie looked at her mother, her eyebrows raised in wonderment.

Sandy bit her lip, struggled, but lost the battle. She began to cry.

Natalie touched her mother's arm. "I'm sorry, Mom. I shouldn't have said anything."

Sandy shook her head, wiping her eyes. "It's okay. We should be able to talk about this. Talking is good for us, right? Besides, who ever said crying is a bad thing? If we don't show how much we miss the people we love, if we never talk about them again—as if they never were part of our lives and hearts—doesn't that seem terrible? I think we need to talk about Robbie more, not less. It's time we let Robbie back into our lives, don't you think?"

Natalie shrugged, tears welling in her own eyes.

After a moment, Sandy continued, "You know, sometimes what we remember about things, or people, isn't so true. I mean, we tend to remember either the *good* things or the *bad* things. Often we don't blend them into what really was. Like when I think of Robbie, I don't think about how aggravating he could be when he latched onto some idea he wanted to make happen; I just think about his laugh, the way he could charm just about anybody, that kind of stuff."

"What do you mean?" asked Natalie.

"Well, everyone in this family has made Robbie out to be some kind of wonderful saint. We all act like his death was the end of the world, and that without him we're nobody, that our lives have all ended too. But, you know Robbie wasn't perfect. He was real. He had his faults as well as his good points. And we can remember him and love him, and use that love to build our lives without letting it hold us back."

Natalie tightened defensively, and Sandy rushed to reassure her.

"Baby, don't take me wrong. When Robbie died part of me died too. I miss him with all my heart. Sometimes it feels like my heart will break when I remember how he used to do this or that." A lump the size of a mountain caught in Sandy's throat, and she struggled to clear it. "But sweetheart, we have to find ways to go on . . ." Glancing at Natalie, she could see the girl's angry frown, her whole body rigid. Obviously, this was *not* what Natalie wanted to hear. Sandy gave up, unsure of what she had been going to say anyway. Silence grew between them again.

A well-kept, classic 1965 green Oldsmobile Cutlass, with a white-haired man at the wheel, came toward them as they rolled off the bridge. Sandy recognized Silas Hobart's prized possession. They waved at each other as the vehicles passed.

Silas was the father of Jeff's first wife, Kathy, and grandfather of the twins. It was Silas who had brought Sandy to Hampton Corner and introduced her to Jeff. For that she would always love the man. Too bad Jeff didn't feel that way about his ex-father-in-law.

Sandy swallowed as realization dawned. If Silas was heading for the farm, tonight's anniversary celebration might be hard to get started.

# c h a p t e r   4

*Where are those twins now?* Jeff, hat in hand, absently scratched at the thin spot developing at the back of his head. Because Jeff had sandy-colored hair, the bald spot was not as noticeable as it would have been on dark-haired men, but he was still sensitive about it. *Dang those two! Seems like they're always wandering off.*

Surveying the pigpens, he saw they had been cleaned. Good, at least they had done *something* he told them to. But that still didn't make up for the boys taking off without checking in first. He sighed deeply, put his hat back on, and resumed looking around the farm, trying to figure out where they might be.

Now, if someone had wanted a stereotypical Midwest farmer, Jeff could have been almost the perfect model. He stood five feet, ten inches tall, and weighed 195 pounds. He had broad shoulders and powerful arms, a legacy from years of weight training for football and wrestling. He also had a slight roll around his middle, attesting to a hearty appetite. He was a strong man, in both body and spirit, and had overcome many odds throughout his life. He was determined, or, as Sandy had said more than once, he was just too darn stubborn to give up. *Stubborn, or just plain stupid?* Jeff had wondered more than once. Maybe it was just plain stupid stubbornness. Whatever it was, it had worked for him, and he saw no reason to change his tactics.

Jeff had always lived in lower Illinois, always been a farm boy, except for the year he went away to a vocational school in Chicago, where he had studied electronics repair. The big city life had been a whole other world. Jeff had just begun finding his feet in that kind of world when his folks decided to retire to Arizona.

His married older brother, with a family of his own and a life no longer connected to the family farm, decided he didn't want the farm. There had been no one else but Jeff to look after the place. They had all talked of selling it, but it had been the family's farm for generations. The idea of selling a part of the family legacy was more than Jeff could bear. So Jeff decided farming was what he wanted after all and changed his path. That was all there was to it. Even with the troubles it brought, and there had been plenty, he rarely thought about the decision after he'd made it, and had never regretted making the choice.

Jeff knew farming was hard and demanding, but he believed whole-heartedly it built character, both in himself and in his family. The sacrifices and commitment of the work made him strong. It was an honest kind of work that few people understood anymore.

While Jeff's belief may have been true, it didn't pay the bills. And the bills attached to farming were enormous. Jeff was deeply in debt and barely able to make his payments. If they could have just a few good years in a row, things would get better. Just a couple of good years was all he needed, just two in a row even. *Please, God!* He sent a small prayer heavenward. *And just where were those boys?!*

"Jason!" yelled Jeff. His son Jason had been born twelve minutes before his identical twin Jarod, a fact Jason never let his "younger" brother forget. Jason was the leader of the two. Wherever Jason was, Jarod wouldn't be far away.

"Jason!" Jeff yelled again. Shaking his head in frustration, he listened with one ear cocked toward the corn-grinding shed, checking on his project for the day while surveying the area. As he listened and looked, Silas Hobart's car came up the drive and stopped at the house.

Jeff's face grew tight, and he frowned deeply. Tiredness washed over him as he watched the old man get out of the car and knock on the front door of the house. It didn't matter to him that Silas was his ex-father-in-law and the twins' grandfather. Nor that Jeff's first wife, Kathy, was Silas Hobart's only child. That was all in the past, and that was where Jeff wanted to leave it. Jeff often wished Silas would just move somewhere far away, or at least leave him and his family alone. But Silas *wouldn't*. The stubborn old man *never* gave up.

Jeff waited and watched. From where he stood between the sheds, he could see Silas without being detected. If the old man left without talking to anyone, that would be best. Jeff was sure their relationship would never get better. Too much hurt, too much history. Way too much water under that particular bridge for either man to ever really venture across.

After taking on the farm Jeff had married Kathy Hobart. Taking over the farm and marrying Kathy had seemed, back then, like the necessary two halves of the whole. A farmer needed a wife.

Actually it hadn't been that simple. Jeff had dated Kathy on the sly off and on through her senior year of high school. Her father hadn't approved because Jeff was not an active church-goer, and was also six years older than Kathy. Jeff adored Kathy and went to great lengths to find gifts to delight her, bringing big and little surprises just to see happiness on her face, to feel her arms around his neck, her sweet kisses on his lips. At times she was demanding, spoiled, and selfish. But in Jeff's young mind that was okay. He was crazy about her, and she deserved to be treated like royalty. She was, after all, her daddy's little princess, and had never gone without.

Kathy had seemed to enjoy the thrill of being loved so ardently by a man her father disapproved of, an "older" man at that. She was an unusually beautiful young woman, sought after and popular—voted prom queen—and she enjoyed telling Jeff about the other boys who wanted her. She would always curl up in his arms then, like a contented kitten, and purr to him how she preferred a "real" man. It had made him feel strong and capable, as if he could conquer the whole world.

Later Jeff would wonder how he could ever have believed she would adapt to the crushing sacrifices of farm life. When he really thought about it, he realized he hadn't thought at all. He had been so blinded by his need for Kathy he hadn't stopped to think it through. He would wonder bitterly why he had been so blind. Later, he would wonder a lot of things.

Jeff was twenty-four back then, and beautiful, vibrant Kathy was eighteen and freshly graduated from high school. Her choice of a husband infuriated her parents, and Silas had done everything he could to stop the marriage. In the end, Jeff often wished Silas had gotten his wish.

The twins were born a year later, and almost a year to the day after that Kathy ran away.

Jeff blamed Silas, and Silas blamed Jeff. That Silas was the LDS bishop of the only ward in the area didn't help Jeff's already weak testimony of the church. He went completely inactive, and hadn't set foot in the church building for the past eighteen years.

Kathy ran as far as she could get, and kept right on running; from time to time calling Jeff, always when life had dealt her some unexpected blow, when some dream had gone up in smoke yet again. When she begged Jeff to come get her, Jeff and his broken heart couldn't refuse her and off he would go to bring her back. But she was always gone when he got there. Eventually Jeff changed his phone number.

A year after Kathy ran away and Silas Hobart had just been called as the new stake president, Jeff finally decided to file for divorce. Silas tried to talk Jeff into dropping the divorce proceedings. He laid it all out how Jeff had done everything wrong, warning him not to make yet another big mistake. The two of them yelled at each other and almost came to blows that night before Jeff ordered Silas off the farm. For a long time after they had behaved as if the other didn't exist.

Sandy Mitchell Soderson MacFarland brought the two men back into each other's lives. Sandy's first husband, Adam, was dying of bone cancer and being treated at the same St. Louis hospital where Silas's wife was being seen for breast cancer. As members of a cancer support group for families, Sandy and Silas met and both filled the void for each other—she filled in for Kathy and played the supportive daughter, while Silas became like a father to the struggling young wife. Tanzie Hobart survived, but Sandy's husband died. Sandy found herself a single mother with a small boy to raise alone, and almost destitute as most of Adam's life insurance money had gone to pay the medical bills. Sandy had a teaching degree she had never used and wasn't sure she would be able to get a job. Her whole life had been her family. She was very much alone, but determined to make it work, somehow. For Robbie's sake, if nothing else.

Sandy had mentioned to Silas that if she couldn't get a teaching job she could always wait tables until she found something better. Silas admired Sandy's courage and had wanted to help her. So he didn't waste any time in arranging a teaching job for Sandy with the Randolph County School District, where he was the superintendent.

As a single father with twin three-year-old boys, Jeff was always looking for someone to help him care for them while he worked the farm. He had gone through a series of sitters and hadn't had much luck with any of them. It seemed to be an ongoing problem that had him stressed out and the boys in turmoil. When Sandy moved to town, she quickly learned about the babysitting situation at the MacFarland place. Being a twin herself, Sandy was always interested in other twins, and eventually contacted Jeff to offer her help. She came to tend the boys sometimes in the evenings after school, and her little Robbie got along well with them. Time passed, one thing led to another, and not quite a year later Sandy asked Jeff to marry her—a request that had stunned Jeff, and he had asked for time to think about it.

The boys loved Sandy, couldn't get enough of her, and Jeff had to admit she could find soft spots in him no one else could. She had won a place in all their hearts, and Jeff honestly couldn't imagine life without her. He finally shook off his hurt over Kathy and did the right thing. Down on one knee, with three dozen roses delivered to their table, and a cheering, clapping group of onlookers around them, Jeff proposed in the middle of a St. Louis restaurant. Sandy had only managed an, "It's about time," before bursting into happy tears in front of their thunderous audience.

Yet Sandy's continuing close friendship with Silas Hobart had complicated things for Jeff. The pushy man was the last person he would ever ask out to the house, although Sandy was quick to point out the twins needed their maternal grandfather, especially with Jeff's parents living so far away and visiting so rarely. She had told him more than once, "Kids need all the love they can get from every stable adult they can get it from. Would you deny your boys the love and support Silas has to offer?" It aggravated him half to death, the more so because he couldn't deny the truth of her statement.

Of course he felt sorry for the Silas. His wife, Tanzie, had died of heart failure a year after Jeff and Sandy had married, her heart weakened by the chemotherapy she had so courageously undergone, and Silas was subsequently released as stake president. So the guy had lost his wife, and his only child was no good. But why did he have to take it upon himself to look after the twins, as well as Sandy and her son Robbie? Jeff was annoyed, especially because he worked hard to make sure his family was well cared for. He didn't need or *want* Silas's help!

To further complicate matters, Sandy seemed to feel the need to look after Silas now that Tanzie was gone. Through all the long months of Tanzie's illness, and eventual death, Sandy was always looking after the couple, calling them, visiting them, taking them dinner. After Tanzie's death, Sandy started asking Jeff to let Silas come to dinner. Jeff wouldn't hear of it. Sandy persisted, and they had the first major fight of their marriage. Sandy invited Silas anyway, and Jeff disappeared the night Silas came. Jeff and Sandy were cool toward each other for weeks after that.

Jeff admitted to himself he probably could have been more mature. After all, when Sandy had wanted to adopt the twins, Silas had helped look for his daughter to sign the papers. Kathy, of course, could not be found. In many ways, Silas had grown closer to Sandy than he ever had to Kathy. Kathy hadn't even shown up for her mother's funeral! By then, Silas was finally resolved that Kathy was not, nor would ever be, the kind of mother the boys so desperately needed.

Jeff supposed part of it was that Silas could talk to Sandy in ways Silas wouldn't let himself talk to anyone else. He lived alone, and that big house of his no doubt felt empty. Sandy told Jeff how Silas had poured out his fears and worries to her, and Sandy had simply listened and understood. In return, Silas filled in for Sandy's deceased father. It made sense. In many ways, Silas and Sandy had many similarities in their lives, both losing people they loved and having to face life alone.

Eventually Jeff gave in a little and managed to simply make himself scarce—always with a reasonable excuse, to temper Sandy's anger—when Silas came out to visit. That was how he dealt with it, and while Sandy didn't like it, she came to accept it. For now anyway, she always told herself. Besides, she could understand Jeff's side too, although she always called him stubborn. Well, maybe he was. And he knew it wasn't always such a good thing to be.

Now, looking at the man standing patiently on the porch, his hat held in his hand, Jeff rolled his eyes. "Shoot," he grumbled, kicking the dirt. For Sandy, and only for Sandy, he would suck it up and make nice. Maybe this would only be a short visit. *Sure, and maybe the price of pork futures would triple by next week.*

Jeff walked slowly toward the house. As Silas turned and caught sight of him, he squared his shoulders. Again, Jeff noticed that Silas looked very much the part of the distinguished patriarch. With thick silver hair topping a tall, slim frame, Silas Hobart was everyone's ideal of the LDS stake president. If Jeff had been really honest, he would've admitted the man rather intimidated him. That intimidation aggravated him and only added to the ill will he felt toward his boys' grandfather.

Coming within hearing distance, Jeff spoke first, "Silas," he nodded at the silver-haired man in acknowledgment.

Silas stepped off the porch and came around the car, stopping a few feet away. "I saw Sandy and Natalie heading across the bridge as I was coming in."

Jeff nodded. "They've gone off on errands. I don't expect them back anytime soon," meaning, *There's nobody here to talk to.* Jeff hoped that would satisfy the old man and send him on his way.

Silas ran a hand through his hair and gazed up at the clear blue sky. "How do the levees look? Think they'll hold?" Silas's question was standard talk lately. Every farmer in the valley between the Hampton River northward to the town of Valmeyer wondered about that very thing.

Jeff shrugged. "Levee District thinks so. I took a look myself yesterday, they seem solid enough. There's some leaks, but I think we'll be okay."

Silas nodded this time. "Corn crop looks good," he observed.

Jeff rubbed his chin, looking over the fields. "Good enough." *What does the old man want?* Jeff glanced pointedly at his watch.

Silas swallowed and fumbled with something in the pocket of his sports coat. Although retired, he still preferred formal dress. "I have a letter here for you. It's from Kathy."

Jeff tightened.

"She wants to come back and see the boys."

Jeff smiled grimly, shaking his head slowly, unable to believe the words. "You know, some things never change. It's kind of like that river over there." His eyes surveyed the long line of huge oak trees along the landward side of the levee. "People know they live by a river that could some day flood them out. But they pretend it won't. And," Jeff kicked a stone away from him, "when it does, they'll scream for everyone to come running and save them from their stupidity."

"She just wants to see them . . ."

"Well that's the tough part about being a runaway parent, isn't it? You just lose out on some things. And the one that's left behind has to pick up all the pieces."

"Please Jeff, it won't be for long; she's not asking for a whole lot." Silas stretched out a pleading hand toward Jeff.

"No way!"

"She has AIDS, Jeff. She's dying." Silas swallowed back the lump in his throat, unwanted tears filling his eyes. He blinked rapidly to keep them from spilling.

Jeff was momentarily stunned, but unrelenting. After a moment, he managed, "I'm sorry for you." He looked out across the cornfields to avoid the pain in Silas's eyes.

"She's here now, back at the house. I brought her back." Silas's eyes watered. "She needs to be with her family at a time like this."

Jeff's whole body was cold.

"It was all a long time ago—" Silas hesitated, tentative.

"You're right, Silas. It *was* all a long time ago. *Too* long. The boys don't need to see her."

"Please, Jeff?"

Silas had never lowered himself this way before. He was actually *begging* Jeff. Jeff felt sorry for him, but that didn't change anything. He shook his head adamantly. "It's history now. It'll only hurt them more. What's the point of opening this all up again? You said yourself she's dying. It might help *her* feel better, but at what cost to *them?* No! That's *final.*"

Silas's eyes tightened, a look of the old hard-charging school superintendent coming over him. "They're old enough to decide for themselves," he threatened stubbornly.

Jeff's temper flashed and he whirled around, his eyes full of fire. "Stay away from them. I'm warning you. She's hurt them enough already. Besides, they aren't her kids anymore, remember? Not legally, not in actuality; not—her—kids!"

Silas stared, searching, unable to find words.

The corn grinder cycled several times, signaling it was almost empty. Jeff looked back at the shed, then at Silas, tempted to order him again off his land. That, however, would have just caused more problems with Sandy, so instead he simply turned and walked away.

He could feel Silas watching him. If he knew what was good for him, he wouldn't follow.

Silas sadly put the letter back into his pocket before walking slowly to the car and getting in. He sat for several minutes, tears coursing freely down his cheeks, before starting up the old car and driving off.

\* \* \*

*Kathy is back. Kathy is back. She's back now, when no one needs her. But where was she when . . .* Jeff left the last thought alone. He stormed through the barnyard, kicking stones out of his way, glaring at everything. One of the cats that liked Jeff, and usually rubbed up against him for attention, took a look at his face and slunk away.

The urge to run away, to hide, to just throw it all away rose in his throat. *Oh, that's stupid,* he thought. *I've got a wife and kids. I have a farm to run. Besides, why should I run away? I haven't done anything wrong!*

*So what about you? Don't you deserve something for all you've done? Haven't you earned some time away?* came the inner voice as he stepped into the barn.

"And when do I ever ask anyone for time off?" he said out loud to himself. "Never! So why can't I—"

*You can't. That's all there is to it,* replied his conscience.

Without warning, the old thirst came over him, the old craving, the deep need.

He blinked, feeling dry-mouthed. *Geez, how long has it been now? Over a year?* He remembered how good it had tasted. Well, at least at first. Toward the end taste wasn't all that important. But at least it had made things bearable. Besides, it never hurt anyone but himself.

*But I promised Sandy I would give it up. And I kept that promise. Unless you want to count those two times . . . no, it was three. I told her about those.* Jeff played with the handle of a pitchfork. *At least I think I did. And we've gotten past all that now. Besides, it's just one little drink. It won't even really count.*

He went over to a toolbox in the corner, and reached far behind, under a pile of old boards. He pulled out the bottle and sighed. *Good. It's still here. Vodka's not my favorite, but at least it doesn't smell so much on my breath.* Jeff lightly shook the bottle, swirling the drink around inside. *Sandy knew I drank when she married me. Shoot, she drank back then too. We used to make those margaritas and sit out on the porch in the evenings. Nothin' wrong with that . . .*

Jeff hesitated, holding the bottle by the neck and looking at the steel barn-pillar beside him. *It would be so easy to smash the bottle and be done with it. No more hiding, no more half-truths. I'm not a good liar. Or am I? This bottle has been out here for over a year.*

He opened it and inhaled. All sorts of memories came flooding back, some of them not so pretty. Like the time he drank for three days after he went looking for Kathy for the first time. It was a good thing the twins were with a friend's family. He'd been so drunk he couldn't even take care of himself, let alone those little ones. And lucky for him that policeman in Nebraska had compassion for a poor, heartbroken fool.

He thought more about Kathy, about the other times he'd tried to drown the pain and disappointment—his anger increasing as she once more opened up old wounds. But in the end, the contents of the bottle were untouched, capped, and hidden back under the boards behind the toolbox.

\* \* \*

While Jeff wondered what foul ball life was going to throw at him next, Jason and Jarod were lying on the hood of the green flatbed truck. It was parked behind the silo, and Jason was reading out loud from a farm magazine, struggling with the larger words from time to time.

"Hog odors are caused by a soup of about 150 gases that result from the bacterial decomposition of manure. The most commonly cited suspects in hog odor, hydrogen sulfide and ammonia, aren't even the worst offenders." As Jason stumbled through the next sentence, Jarod yawned, bored. He settled his ball cap tightly over his eyes and wriggled a bit in hopes of finding a more comfortable position in which to enjoy the pleasantly warm sun.

Jason ignored the yawn and kept right on with the article. "The odors come from three sources: from the barns themselves, from crop lands where the wastes are sprayed, and from the lagoons where the wastes are stored. The gases that cause hog odor tend to travel in a plume, or clump, and are just as concentrated 1,500 feet from the barn as they are just outside the barn."

"Quit. I can't stand it anymore." Jarod covered his ears and moaned loudly to make his point.

"Roofing shingles, siding, fabrics, and other materials can act as a 'sink' for hog odors, trapping the compounds at night and releasing them during the day as the sun beats down. Fatty tissues in the human body absorb the compounds in the same way, Schiffman said."

"I bet Dad doesn't know this stuff," Jason said as he read parts of the article again.

Uncovering his ears, Jarod said, "I bet he don't care, either. How come you do?"

Jason rolled up the magazine. "I don't know. It's just interesting to me. Better than shoveling hog crap forever."

Jarod leaned over and shoved his brother off the hood of the truck. "Might as well get used to it, 'cause that's all you're ever going to do."

From the ground, Jason glared at his "little" brother. Grabbing Jarod's leg, he yanked him off the truck. In a flash the two of them were wrestling on the ground.

A moment later, water splashed down on the two boys. Sputtering and yelling in surprise, they looked up to find their dad, anger in his face and an empty bucket in his hands.

"Where've you two been? Do I have to keep track of you all the time?"

"But Dad, we got the pens done," defended Jarod.

"You didn't say there was anything else we needed to do this morning," added Jason.

"We were just takin' a break, Dad. We worked *hard* today." said Jarod.

"When are you two going to grow up? You know you're supposed to check back with me when you're done, to see what else needs doing." Exasperated, Jeff dropped the bucket with a clunk. "Get over to the feed barn and bring me some more corn for grinding."

"What's got into *him?*" Jason asked no one in particular, watching his father disappear around the corner of the barn.

"Beats me," replied his twin, standing up and trying in vain to brush off the worst of the mud he was now spattered with. "But you know when he acts like that there's no use arguin'. Come on, first one to the barn gets to haul while the other loads!" And stretching out one long arm, Jarod smacked his older brother in the back of the head before racing off with a holler and a laugh, Jason coming up fast behind him.

Stomping off, Jeff shook his head at them. Maybe he had been a little unfair to them. But dang! Those two never seemed to take anything seriously for more than a minute. They could be annoying in the best of times, but now, since Silas's disturbing news, they were unbearable. Jeff began to stew over what would happen when Sandy found out about Kathy. Instead of fighting with Sandy over Silas, they'd probably start fighting over Kathy and the twins. That Sandy. She was one hard woman to figure out. Most women would be tickled pink their husband wanted nothing to do with his ex-wife. But not Sandy. She was always worrying about doing the right thing for everybody, showing mercy and forgiveness and all that garbage. Wasn't life already hard enough without that?

Jeff was angry, but he was also unsure of what would happen next. If he were completely honest with himself, he would admit he was just plain *scared*. He wasn't exactly sure of what. But he knew one thing for sure, he didn't like being scared one bit.

\* \* \*

Starting his first assignment from Mike, John looked inside one of the air conditioners he'd been told to clean and asked his self-appointed assistant, "Where do I find a wire brush?"

Scooter thought for a moment, then skipped off, returning a moment later with one. John began cleaning off the debris that had accumulated on the conditioner baffles. "How many rooms in this place?" he asked.

"Fifty-seven," Scooter quickly recited from memory. "Twenty smoking, and the rest not. My mom doesn't want any of them to be smoking ones, but Mike says that isn't real."

"Too bad people smoke, huh?"

"Yeah. Mike used to smoke, but he quit. I heard him tell my mom that was the hardest part about joining the Church."

John put down the wire brush, and after blowing on the baffles, took a sponge from a bucket of soapy water and began wiping them off. "Like the bumper sticker says, 'Be Smart, Don't Start.'" John grinned at Scooter, who grinned right back up at him. Reaching in even deeper with the brush to get a particularly sticky bit of dirt, John continued, "So Scooter, do you like going to church?"

Scooter scrunched up his face. "Yeah, most of the time, but sometimes it's boring. I like primary though, 'cause we get to sing songs with *all* the actions and play games and stuff. My mom really likes church. She says it keeps her alive. I'm not really sure what she means by that, but I think it means she likes it."

John glanced at the boy and nodded, understanding. Smells from the nearby hamburger place drifted in the air, and a cat in the park across the street spooked pigeons off the statue of the town's Civil War hero. It was a regular day, a beautiful day, and John was glad to be alive and enjoying it.

Out of sight, across the compound on the balcony of the café, Mike watched John and Scooter. He had originally gone up there to look at the water level on the river side of the levee again. This morning he had found some wet spots behind the motel beside the earthen retaining wall that abutted the levee. The wetness hadn't been there last week. Maybe it was just from the heavy rain the past few days, Mike observed, but maybe it wasn't. When he got a chance, he would ask someone about it. It worried him, but he was trying to shrug it off. *It's probably no big deal,* he tried to tell himself. He was afraid of looking like a needless worrier or, worse, as if he had no *machismo. Old habits die hard,* he thought to himself, embarrassed that he was even concerned about it.

Scooter and the new guy were sure talking a lot. It surprised Mike because Scooter didn't warm up very fast to anyone. And here he was, shooting the breeze with John after a couple days. Mike discovered that if he leaned precariously far over the railing, he could just hear what they were talking about. He felt a little guilty doing it, but he couldn't help himself. He was fascinated by John. There was just something about the guy that drew people to him. Mike wanted to know what it was.

Meanwhile, down in the office, a disgruntled customer was complaining to Linda about his room. His loud voice carried easily up to Mike, who felt torn between wanting to hear John and Scooter's conversation, and getting down below to help his wife with the difficult situation.

"I like church myself." John continued, as he checked the loose air-conditioner covering and found a loose screw. "It's relaxing." He winked at Scooter. "How about a Phillips screwdriver now?"

Scooter looked thoughtful. "Are those the ones that look like stars, kind of?"

"Yup."

Scooter was gone in a flash.

With the boy gone, John settled back off his crouched legs to sit against the wall under the window. He closed his eyes, feeling the quiet. He thought about Mike and Linda, how much energy they spent worrying about each other and the place—how much time they lost in the little things when they could just be enjoying each other and Scooter. And without searching for it, a memory slid up from his long-ago past.

*A gathering, a large meal, with many conversations. The last bit of setting sun was coming across the Sea of Galilee and peeking into the courtyard. Jesus was smiling and talking softly with Simon Peter's wife and mother. Some were affectionately teasing Peter about how he snored when he was really tired. Peter made a good-humored face at his wife, then took another bite of broiled fish.*

*John sat, watching Jesus and learning how to be happier. He needed the lesson; John had been so intense most of his life. The Lord's reprimand of John and his brother, for wanting to call down fire on a village of people who would not hear the truth, still stung.*

*"Ye know not what manner of spirit ye are of," He had said. "For the Son of man is not come to destroy men's lives, but to save them."* [2]

*The message was clear. The hostile villagers were as beloved by their Father as His disciples. There was still time for them. And at that moment John realized he was young and lacked wisdom.* I still have much to learn about life, and perfection, *he thought.*

*Watching while Jesus hugged Peter good-naturedly, John began to understand.*

*"Life is best lived with a smile and a laugh," John whispered to himself.*

*As if he had heard John's words, Jesus stopped His conversation with Peter and looked across the room to where John sat, then nodded. The Master knew John was beginning to understand at last.*

*The Savior had later enumerated John's thoughts: "Be of good cheer; I have overcome the world."* [3] *And with that knowledge, John could be of good cheer—no matter what happened.*

"Here's the screwdriver," said Scooter.

John's eyes focused back to the present. "Ah, good. Let's get back to work."

"You okay?" asked Scooter. "Your face was kind of weird."

John ruffled the kid's hair. "Just remembering a good time, long ago. Just reminding myself to keep a smile on my face, to appreciate what I've got right here and now."

"Yeah," the boy nodded. "Mom says, 'There is no situation so bad that a bad attitude can't make worse.'"

"Very true," confirmed John. "You have one smart mom, my man."

In a few minutes, finished with the repair, John pocketed the screwdriver, picked up the brush and bucket, and moved on to the next room. "One down, only fifty-six more to go." Taking the air-conditioner cover off, he began to clean.

After working silently for a time, John asked, "So, you live here at the motel?"

Scooter nodded. "Yup. Mom wants a house, but Mike says we have to get the motel doing better first. My mom's aunt didn't do much with it before, so now it needs a lot of work. That's what Mike says."

"So, that's who owned it before your folks did?"

Scooter hung out over the railing, balancing himself, and could have seen Mike across the way if he had been looking. Mike pulled back inside.

"My mom's aunt died and left her the motel. Before that we were living in Chicago. I had to go to school at this real creepy place. One of the teachers kept a gun in his desk. He wasn't supposed to, but he did. I was glad when we left. I like it here. It's lots better."

John smiled, then frowned as he heard yelling from the office. He stood, listened, then dropped the wire brush beside the bucket. "Sounds like your mom needs some help. Why don't you hang out here for a minute while I go check it out?" Without waiting for Scooter's answer, John hurried toward the escalating voice.

* * *

"I'm not paying a penny to this flea-bag pit!" yelled the large man in the office. A veritable cloud of foul breath spewed from the man. He stank of cigarettes, onions, stale whiskey, and unwashed body—a product of too many days on the road trucking and not enough bathing. Linda winced at the odor.

Turning her head slightly away to escape the stink, Linda remained calm. "Well, our night manager *should* have required you to pay in advance. But, if you could just tell me what precisely it was you disliked, then perhaps we can do whatever we need to do to make it better for you and everyone else who comes here in the future."

"That's *your* problem, *you* figure it out. *I* shouldn't have to tell you what's wrong with it. It's *your* job to make it decent for honest, hardworking folks like me! This place is a *dump* and oughta be condemned!" More profanity poured out of his mouth. "If it weren't on the river road north, nobody would even come to this one-horse town. And if I hadn't been so dead tired last night, I would've seen that and not even stopped. But I can see it clear as a bell now, and I'm not paying *you* anything."

John slipped silently in the office door, and stood behind the man, who was a head taller and a good seventy pounds heavier.

"Look, you did sleep here, so we provided you a service—" continued Linda.

"Forget it. I'm not paying!" The man turned, and immediately ran into John.

John smiled.

"You're in my way." The man glared threateningly down at John.

John held out his hands placatingly. "Oh no, we can't let you go without making things up to you, sir. We'd hate to lose a good customer like yourself."

The man leaned down toward John. "Get *out* of my way, shorty."

"How about a cash payment for your trouble?"

Linda couldn't believe her ears. She glared at John. Just what did he think he was doing?

For the first time, the big man eased up a bit, eyeing John suspiciously, but with interest. "What's the catch?"

"No catch. You aren't satisfied, so we'll make you happy. Then perhaps you'll change your mind about this motel and tell all your friends what a great place we run here. Good for you, good for business, good for us. Right, Linda?" John looked at Linda and winked.

Linda protested, "But he didn't—"

John moved around the man and gently touched Linda's arm, looking into her eyes as he spoke to her. "No, he didn't pay anything, and he shouldn't if he feels the way he does. We can pay him some money to ease the discomfort he so obviously had to endure. Besides," John shrugged, "he's going to need it pretty quickly."

It took a moment for John's meaning to sink in.

"What are you talking about?" demanded the man.

"Well, that's your rig parked around back, isn't it?"

"Yeah. So what?"

"I noticed your plates are expired. And from the way your tires look, I'll bet you're running too heavy a load for this state. The sheriff wouldn't like that if he caught you. Might even let you cool your heels at his place while he calls up your company boss." John scratched his chin. "I noticed your load isn't sealed anymore, either. Could it be someone took something out of there that they weren't supposed to? And I hate to say it, but you look a bit like you might have been drinking . . . there are some empty bottles in the cab of your truck. Add it all together and it just doesn't look good. No sir. Not a good day for you at all, I'd guess."

The angry man's tone shifted. "You . . . you've been prowlin' 'round my truck! What gives you the right?" He started to sweat.

John continued, "Well, it's part of my job here to keep an eye on things. Safety precautions, you know. And it just seems like your trouble is doubling by the moment. I bet your boss won't be very pleased you didn't make it to Chicago yesterday. Still, maybe he'll believe your story about engine trouble. Then again, maybe not, especially if the sheriff takes it into his head to call about these other concerns too."

The trucker knew he was beat.

"Linda, after we pay this guy for staying here, why don't you give the sheriff's office a call? You could talk to them real nice and vouch for our friend here. You know, explain what a great guy he is. Just kind of forgetful and all . . . probably has had a lot on his mind and such. . . ."

The trucker looked at Linda, then back at John. He was *really* mad, yet he was also smart enough to know it was over. Finding forty dollars in his wallet, he tossed the money on the counter in front of Linda. "There. That oughta cover whatever you charge for this rip-off joint."

"You know," said John, "I hope the sheriff is in a good mood today. He's been suffering from migraines a lot lately, and they make him kind of cranky. Maybe when you call, Linda, you can ask how he's feeling and give us an idea of where our friend here might stand."

Glaring at John, the trucker found fifty dollars more in his wallet. "Will this do?"

John picked up the money. "Well gosh, this is way more than what your room cost! Are you sure you feel okay with this? I mean, normally folks don't tip us near this much."

"Keep it. Give it to charity. I don't care." The defeated driver quickly pushed his way out of the office.

"Wait," John called after the guy. "Thank you, but really, this is too much." The driver began to run. Without even looking back, he waved John off, climbed into his truck, and started it up, leaving town as fast as his rig would let him.

"Make sure you don't forget to bring your wife that special craft paint she wants from St. Louis," called John as the truck swept by him. "Otherwise there'll be trouble when you get home."

John walked back into the office and shrugged as he handed the money to Linda. "Guess this is yours too."

Laughing incredulously, Linda shook her head. "Nope, the extra we give to someone who needs it more than we do. Remember? He said to give it to charity!"

Leaning back to open the glass door of the office, Mike clumsily made his way in. It had taken Mike much longer than he intended to get down the stairs and around the complex to the office. He grimaced in pain as the crutches dug into his underarms. "What happened?"

"No problem, Mike. John took care of it. Most amazing thing I ever saw!" Linda grinned, her eyebrows raised in delight.

"Took care of what?" Mike felt irritated. After all, it wasn't John's place to rescue *his* wife.

"He got us paid." Linda held up the money. "With a donation for the poor, to boot."

Mike frowned in disbelief. "From that trucker? I could hear him complaining all the way over in the café. What exactly did you *do* to that guy?" he asked John in amazement.

John grinned and shrugged at Mike. "Nothing, really. I just pointed out what a great deal he was getting here. Guess maybe he had a guilty conscience or something," John explained. "Well, excuse me, I gotta get back to work. I've got a bunch more air-conditioning units waiting for me."

As the office door shut behind John, Linda giggled again and said, "Good man you hired there, boss."

Mike snorted as Linda put the money away. "*I* hired? If I recall, it was Scooter who had the most to do with it. And then you and Charlene. I know who the *real* bosses are around here, no matter what anybody *says*. And speaking of Charlene, what's gotten into her?"

"Charlene?"

"Yes, Charlene. She's acting really weird. I didn't hear her growl once this morning. When I came in for breakfast she was all fancied up. She smiled at me and wished me a good morning. She was *singing*."

"It's John. I told you, she's got a crush on him."

Mike rolled his eyes. "You were really serious? No kidding!"

Linda smiled like the Cheshire cat. "She may be older, but she's still a woman. And John *is* kind of cute."

Before Mike could reply, Linda came out around the counter and took her husband's arm. "But of course, he hasn't got your dashing good looks. *Nobody* holds a candle to *you*. That reminds me, my own gorgeous guy, a new temple preparation class starts this Sunday. How's about you and I take a look at it?"

The temple was a sticky point between Mike and Linda. She wanted more than anything to be sealed to him and have Scooter sealed to them both. With the baby coming, her feelings about eternal families had increased tenfold. Mike, on the other hand, felt uneasy about yet another step deeper into the Church. His memories about religion in Mexico were proving hard to shake. The two churches were in many ways very different, but the emotions even the *word* "church" evoked were sometimes difficult for him to overcome. He loved Linda though, and didn't want to hurt her, but he had to know for himself or he'd feel somehow dishonest about going to the temple and making the promises he was told he'd be making. He wasn't exactly sure what they entailed, but they were sure to be something serious.

Mike wriggled uncomfortably and looked away from her searching eyes. "Maybe."

Linda chewed the inside of her cheek, wanting to say more, but afraid of pushing too hard. "Will you pray about it with me? Please?"

Mike shrugged ambiguously. Changing the subject quickly he said, "I, uh, found something out back. The ground's kind of wet back there."

"Couldn't we just take a look at the class?" she persisted, her eyes full of hope.

"We'll see," he finally answered. Then, after a quick kiss on her forehead, he left the office.

"Please, Lord," whispered Linda. "Please touch his heart. Life is so short."

Mike saw her mouth the words on his way around the building, and for one moment her expression of faith stopped him. It meant so much to her—this eternal marriage thing. And Mike knew she meant as much to him. "We'll see," he said again, but this time for himself.

She went back to her work behind the counter, automatically turning on the radio on the shelf.

"Authorities are now predicting that St. Louis will weather the heavy flooding," said the radio announcer. "But some experts say that the levee protection there will only create greater pressure on places further downstream as the water level rises."

Linda frowned, thinking how Hampton Corner was one of the places down river from St. Louis, right in a critical spot. Great. Just great.

# chapter 5

It was like a bug buzzing in her ear. She couldn't see the darn thing long enough to catch it, but it wouldn't go away when she swatted at it. Sandy just couldn't catch her thought and pin it down, but it wouldn't go away, either. And unlike with a bug, she couldn't even swat at this one. It felt like it was right in her face and her hands were tied. All she could do was get through this, somehow. Sandy could feel her stomach doing flip-flops. *What if it were true?*

"You *had* already heard, hadn't you?" asked Muriel Hobson, holding the package in her hands. Muriel ran the small post office in Hampton Corner and was the worst gossip in the county. Sandy usually avoided her, but today she had no choice. As soon as Jeff's package was safely in her hands though, she would be out of there.

*So, what am I supposed to do?* Sandy asked herself. Even if it were true, saying anything about it publicly would just bring on more problems for the family. Sandy shook her head, not trusting herself to reply. *It can't be true. It makes no sense! Why now, after all these years?*

Muriel's eyes glowed with delight over this juicy bit of news. "Oh goodness, dear, I didn't mean to be the one to drop the bomb on you! I never thought it would ever happen. Imagine, Kathy Hobart, coming back here. Jeff will be fit to be tied. That girl really put him through the wringer." Muriel looked positively transported at the thought of what Jeff might do.

Sandy tried to stop herself. Asking questions only fueled Muriel, but the words popped out on their own. "How did you hear this?"

Muriel looked victorious, obviously pleased that she finally got one up on the usually standoffish Sandy MacFarland. "I have my sources," she preened. "Besides, her father is probably so glad to get her back he's told most of Illinois. I'm surprised you didn't know before now."

Sandy thought of some inappropriate comments about gossips, and took the package from Muriel. "Yeah. See ya," she said, then thought, *Oh Lord, this is all we need. Please, don't let it be true!*

When Sandy climbed back into the truck, Natalie was already there after having quickly checked out the newest magazines at the tiny general store next door. The store still didn't stock *Writer's Digest,* even though Natalie had practically begged them. Maybe she was going to have to give in and order a subscription for herself.

Natalie couldn't help noticing the tight look on her mother's face. "Did the wrong package come?"

Sandy absently shook her head, having to push through all the colliding thoughts. "How stupid can people be?" she muttered.

"What's the matter, Mom?" asked Natalie.

"Nothing, honey, it's the right package." With great effort she tried to clear her face and managed to give Natalie a stiff smile. Sandy considered how this news would effect Jeff, true *or* false. Plant it in his ear, and what would she get? Another swamp of misery, anger, pain, and self-pity most likely. She had already lived with enough of that.

When she could have used Jeff's comfort after Robbie's death, was he around for her? No. Too many nights she had cried herself to sleep, alone. In the end, she found it easier to lock all her feelings about Robbie away deep in her heart. She had told herself Jeff cared—she *knew* he did. He was just the kind of man who hated deep, painful emotion. Instead of reaching out when he was hurting, instead of opening up, Jeff turned his back to the world, hiding his pain. And he handled others' pain the same way.

So Sandy had done the same, at least with him, about Robbie. She reasoned Jeff wouldn't come back to her until she did. And when Jeff saw her smiling again, he turned toward her once again. Over time, it often seemed as if Robbie were a dream between them, one they never acknowledged. It made her feel sick to think about it. Jeff handled the "Kathy thing," as Sandy called it in her own mind, the same way.

"You know, I think we should go get some ice cream at the café."

Natalie's eyes widened. Her mother never went out for something like that. Sometimes she had caught her mother guiltily sneaking ice cream at home, after her parents had fought about something. But not once had she ever taken Natalie *out* for ice cream.

"Maybe even a hot fudge sundae."

Natalie nodded, too stunned to speak. *What's going on with Mom?*

While they were gorging themselves at the Starbright Café, Sandy stopped to lick her long-handled spoon. "I need to make a phone call and check on a friend. Be right back."

Natalie watched her mother as she stepped out to the phone booth just across the street. Soon Sandy's connection went through, and she started talking. She smiled, frowned, bit her lip, shook her head, threw her arm up in exasperation, and basically went through every expression Natalie knew. Whatever she was talking about on the pay phone, it was something important. If only Natalie had learned to lip-read like that deaf boy who'd moved to town two years ago! Natalie frowned, trying to decipher just what was going on.

Charlene, the café cook, came out and swept the sidewalk not far from the phone. Sandy turned her back toward Charlene, as if to cover her phone conversation. *What is going on?!* Natalie wondered.

When Sandy hung up she looked determined, and a little scared. Silas had confirmed the rumor about Kathy coming back. That meant a showdown between Jeff and Kathy over the twins. Well, too bad. Old grudges *needed* to be flushed down the toilet. You just had to hope they didn't plug up the current plumbing in the process.

*That wasn't a pretty image*, she thought, pushing open the phone booth door. *This grudge thing Jeff has against Kathy is really getting thin. Why couldn't he and Kathy just do the* Reader's Digest *condensed version of life—cut through all the garbage and end it peaceably? Can't he see it hurts all the people he says he's trying to protect? All that nuclear fallout just radiating for miles around the two of them, all that pain . . . all that waste of energy and life! Hmmph!* Sandy grinned wryly to herself. *I'm a fine one to talk. It's not* my *past we're worrying about now, is it?*

"Your friend okay?" Natalie looked up at her anxiously.

For a few seconds Sandy didn't understand. "What? Oh, sure. They've been . . . sick for a while. But, I think things will be getting better now." She settled back into the café's booth, and picked up her spoon, diving back into her dessert.

*Doing things openly*, thought Sandy, *would be a good way to start something new. It isn't any sin to be stupid, unless you choose to stay that way. Jeff has just got to examine what's been lost, accept it, and go on from there. He's got to realize someday, somehow, that he's stuck in the past. Shoving the garbage under the bed doesn't make it go away, it just stinks up the bedroom until you're willing to haul it out.*

Sandy grinned to herself. She liked that metaphor. On the farm they made garbage into compost to build a richer soil to plant in. As she thought about it, it seemed life was really like compost. Take the painful stuff and make it into something good to grow from. After all, Sandy reflected, she'd never met anyone who hadn't been hurt by life one way or another. Yet it wasn't the hurt that mattered so much as what you chose to do with it.

Sandy finished her ice cream a split second before her daughter. Then she frowned again, her thoughts wandering back to the current situation. *So, you really think Jeff is going to open up and put his hurt on display for everyone to see? All in the name of health and growth? Ha, fat chance! Dream on, Sandy!*

She determinedly smoothed out her frown lines and smiled again for her daughter. "Let's go, kiddo. I want to swing by the store and pick up something extra special for tonight. I think I'm going to need it."

Natalie nodded, wondering if her mom was aware of how many emotions Natalie had just seen in her face. By now Natalie was dying to know what was going on.

Sandy rolled her eyes as she continued her internal conversation. *Who am I kidding? I could bake all night and that wouldn't do it. There isn't enough food in the whole world to smooth this one over!*

"Mom? Are you okay?" asked a bewildered Natalie.

Startled, Sandy pulled herself together and gave Natalie a reassuring hug. "Sure, honey. I'm okay. Everything is going to be okay." *One way or another . . .*

* * *

Raymond Floyde waited patiently on his knees, listening for an answer to his prayer. He had concerns, and had shared them with the Lord. Now he had to listen for an answer. And, according to what

Raymond had read from Brigham Young, if he didn't quite get one, then he would do the best he could with the light and knowledge he currently had. In this case, he sincerely hoped he wouldn't be left to go it on his own. He really *could* use some inspiration. Things were way over his head this time around.

As deputy sheriff, especially the undersheriff, Raymond was paid to make things happen, or in some cases, not let them happen. He completely believed the old maxim that people who "fail to plan, plan to fail." So he spent a good deal of his time thinking, figuring, and planning about lots of things. And right now, he had more to think about than he cared to shoulder alone.

Kneeling beside his bed, his thoughts wandered a bit. He could still taste the Diet Pepsi from the lunch he had just shared with his wife, Jane. She was Raymond's best friend, and every working day he made it a point to try to come home for lunch. He gave himself a mental shake, pulling his thoughts back into a quiet meditation, waiting for an answer. The answer he received was that the Lord loved him and had confidence in him. Not exactly what Raymond was looking for, but, he acknowledged, a whole lot better than nothing. At least the Lord had heard Raymond and was aware of his concerns.

A quiet man, Raymond nonetheless passionately wanted to make a difference in people's lives, so his job as undersheriff and his calling as second counselor in the Waterloo Ward bishopric were both deeply satisfying. He didn't mind that the members were scattered all over the countryside and that the ward office and meetings were miles away in Waterloo. Although it was a small ward, the boundaries were quite far flung compared with what they would be in another place. He knew in Utah the wards were only a few blocks apart, with meeting houses within walking distance of each other. But that was a different world, one he could only dimly imagine. Life was not like that out here in "the mission field." The members were few and far between, but Raymond felt that only pulled them all the closer. Physical proximity didn't necessarily make for close feelings between people—as Raymond well knew from personal experience.

He sighed deeply, easing back on tired knees. Obviously today there weren't going to be any "marching orders" from the Man Upstairs.

When he walked into the kitchen, Jane put down the towel she was wiping her hands with and leaned back against the counter to look up into his face. "So, what was the answer?"

Raymond shrugged. "I think it was, 'Be still, and know that I am God.'"

Jane smiled up at him, wrapping her arms around his waist. "I've always liked that one."

Nuzzling his face into her soft hair, he pulled her close to him. "Me too, but I could sure use more than that today. That feeling about the levees won't leave me alone. I ran up to Valmeyer this morning and talked to Dave Mosely. He's the head guy there from the Army Corps of Engineers. He was worried. He's not saying that, but I can tell. And when a guy like *that* is worried, then a guy like *me* better be too."

Jane kissed him lightly on the cheek. "Don't worry, it'll come when you really need it. It always does. Remember, God doesn't make mistakes!"

As Raymond gave her another hug and kissed her cheek, Jane remembered something else. Pushing away gently, she locked eyes with him.

"Hey, don't forget, we've got that Young Women's thing tonight in Waterloo."

Raymond immediately thought of the winding, fifteen-mile back road to the town where the ward building was located. "What?"

"Honey, we talked about it last Sunday."

"Oh yeah, that's right. I forgot."

"I can guarantee your three daughters haven't. They're busy right now on a service project, but they expect their father to be at this gathering tonight. No matter what. Their mother, that's different. They see a lot more of me than they do of you."

"Okay, okay. Point made. I'll get out of the town meeting just as soon as I can. I may be a little late, but you can assure my lovely daughters I'll be there."

After he drove off from the house, Raymond pulled over into the small county park where he could look out over Hampton Creek. From where he sat, the view extended all the way to Valmeyer. He could just make out the tall trees up that way. The afternoon was turning hot and muggy with heavy clouds moving in, threatening to pour down even more rain. The ground was already soggy, unable to absorb much more moisture.

Raymond pulled a red, old-style handkerchief from his back pocket and wiped his forehead. His eyes ached. The view wasn't as clear as it had been a year ago. His vision was changing, and he wondered if he would need glasses soon. He shook his head and muttered, "Must be getting old."

Thoughts about work, planning, strategy, and analysis took turns in his head.

*Are we doing what we're supposed to be, Lord? Or are we missing something important we'll regret later?* The thought nagged at him.

The answer was coming down the river, and sooner than he thought.

\* \* \*

That Saturday evening, John and Scooter stood at the back of the combination lunchroom/gym of the Hampton Corner Elementary School. A town meeting was underway, with maybe forty of the residents attending. John was lost in thought, observing the interactions of the residents. He was thinking how the four general approaches to life were represented in this group, as they nearly always were in any large gathering of people.

One small group of people were busy clarifying the problems they were facing as a community and the best way to fix those problems. They saw the potential flood as a challenge to be met and overcome. These were the logical problem solvers of the group, looking for answers in a cut-and-dried manner.

Then there was the group who urged that the needs of people were more important than the needs of the physical community. These folks were also problems solvers, but more compassionate, more willing to get into the "shades of gray" solutions, looking out for individuals, as well as the community, to be sure no one fell through the cracks.

Another group spoke of the government's obligation, local or federal, to step in and take over, to protect what was theirs. They felt they had earned that protection by contributing to the community, paying taxes, and voting. They were hard workers, responsible, black-and-white thinkers who day to day, kept the town rolling on many levels, but in an emergency, waited for a "higher power" to take control and tell them what to do.

Last of all were the rationalizers, who felt sure that somehow, someway, the situation would all be fine and that the flood threat was all being blown out of proportion. This same group made the town get-togethers fun, the people who so often reminded everyone of the sparkle and joy of life. But they didn't do much when it came to the hard decisions and the follow-through; they weren't exactly what you'd call responsibility junkies.

John marveled again at God's wisdom. Within every individual was a part of these four traits, and when all four were blended together as God intended, a formidable human being emerged. Indeed, John believed that was one of the major purposes of this life, to give every individual the opportunity to learn to balance their weaknesses and strengths into one healthy, powerful whole. That seldom happened, as folks were more likely to stick with one view-point, one response to life's challenges, and allow others to help balance out situations by adding their preferred method of action. But that's where God's wisdom came in—providing opportunities for His children to learn from each other.

When folks were willing to combine their view with those of others, working together for the well-being of the whole, great things could come to pass. But so often, the lack of vision and humility stemmed the potential of compromise.

John realized it wasn't a lack of caring or goodness that caused people to act this way; it was an understandable reaction to the unknown. Fear and anxiety caused people to withdraw into the behaviors they knew and understood best, unwittingly making situations worse, not better. And that was exactly what was happening at this meeting.

Dave Mosely, the Army Corps of Engineers representative, had been trying to get his point across for more than an hour. Now he was really exasperated. "I didn't say the levees absolutely *would* fail, I just said *if.*" He waved his arms emphatically, struggling to persuade his audience and still keep his temper. "At this point, *nobody knows* what will happen for sure when the flood waters hit those levees full force. So far, they're holding."

"We all know the levee up at Valmeyer is already leaking. So why aren't you out there doing something to *stop* it before it breaks open and really causes us grief?" called a hostile voice from the rear of the room.

John peered over heads trying to locate the last speaker. She was a tall, stout woman, standing belligerently in the middle of the aisle, hands on hips, looking as if she could bite nails in half. She appeared to be in no mood to be reasoned with, he noted wryly. Poor Dave. John shook his head in silent sympathy. Not an easy crowd to play to tonight.

Dave threw up his hands. "We're doing all that's humanly possible under the circumstances. Crews are working as we speak to sandbag and reinforce those levees in Valmeyer. But you have to understand, there are no guarantees in this kind of emergency work. Levees are delicate structures, and none of them around here were made to withstand the kind of water that's coming down the river now." He picked up a report on the table behind him and quickly glanced at it. "Flood waters at St. Louis should peak by tomorrow, at forty-nine and a half feet." He dropped the report back down on the table. "Flood stage in St. Louis starts at thirty feet, and the flood walls are designed for only fifty. Those are the most massive walls on the whole river, and they're just barely going to make it. If the levees upriver in Quincy hadn't buckled and sucked a lot of the water back that way . . . I don't know where we'd be right now. And that's what I've been trying to explain. There are no certain answers in all this. We just have to try to be as prepared as we can for whatever may happen."

"What exactly are you doing to keep *us* safe?" asked someone else.

"I want to say first, that these levees weren't built by our corps— not that we aren't trying to save them anyway. But, they weren't built to our specifications. And because they weren't, I can't predict exactly what will happen to them." There was an angry murmur in the crowd; clearly, most folks felt this was an unacceptable response from the man they viewed as a representative of their federal government.

A man in the back of the room a little way from John jumped up waving his fist in the air. "So what you're saying is, you're not doing *anything* and we're basically on our own, is that it?" The crowd began to murmur once again. Dave shook his head helplessly, at a loss for words.

Raymond hopped up out of his chair and stepped to the front of the room next to Dave. Holding his hand up, he waved for quiet, stepping in before the crowd got any uglier. "Hold on everybody. I didn't ask Mr. Mosely here just so's we could blame him for the flood. He's doing his best to help us out. Let's not forget we're all on the same side here. We're going to have to try working as a team. If we can do that, we'll get a whole lot farther a whole lot faster. Okay?"

"Nobody's blaming anyone," said a man in the front row. "We just want some clear answers for a change!" There were nods and mutters of agreement from others in the crowd.

Raymond frowned at the man. "Well now, Bob, like Mr. Mosely was just saying, there *are* no really clear answers. Only God knows for sure what's going to happen here, and as far as I know, *He* isn't telling anyone. That right, Pastor?" Raymond called out to Pastor Davis, sitting on the third row. Pastor Davis smiled and shook his head. "He hasn't said anything specific to me, Deputy Floyde." A few folks chuckled, and John grinned, admiring the skillful way Raymond was injecting a little humor into the otherwise tense situation.

Raymond nodded and went on, "That's what I thought. Now you be sure and tell us if you hear something along those lines, won't you, sir? In the meantime, I reckon the good Lord wants us to work on helping ourselves as best we can. Mr. Mosely is here to help us organize ourselves, so when the creek starts rising we'll know what we need to do and be able to do it well."

"Forget the creek! We can handle that. We've done it before, by ourselves, and been just fine," came a call from the back. "We don't need a bunch of outsiders telling us what to do." Once again murmuring voices drifted across the room, some agreeing, some alarmed.

"No! You can't afford to forget the creek." Dave strode forward again, clearly alarmed. "The creek and the river are intertwined in ways that will affect how the flood is going to impact here. This won't be like other times," he said, shaking his head and striding back and forth across the front of the gym in agitation. "You've *never* seen a flood like this one before. Once those levees break—if they break—the water just roars out and keeps coming at you. You can't catch your breath for a moment. I was up at Quincy when it broke through." He stood, hands held out as if pleading for them to understand what he was trying so desperately to show them. "Everything we do, everything we can do, every little bit . . ."

He turned away from them all, running a hand through his hair, obviously stressed.

From the back of the room, John could see what the others didn't seem to. He could see the deep pain in the engineer's heart, the kind that comes from caring, sweating, and giving up pieces of yourself, and still not making any difference. This was more than just another job to Dave Mosely, and it was obvious to John that Dave felt responsible for not having any better answers.

"Can I say something?" came a calm, clear voice above the hubbub.

Everyone craned around in their seats, looking toward the back of the gym. Linda recognized John's voice, and put a hand on Mike's shoulder to steady herself as she shifted around in her seat to look.

"I'm new here," said John. His voice was steady and low, very different from the voices heard in the meeting all evening. "And almost none of you know me. Guess maybe some of you would call me a drifter." An old man, checking out John's blue jeans, sandals, and collar-length hair, frowned in disdain.

"I was up north, in Des Moines, when the water peaked there. And you know, I was really impressed with how those people pulled together and made a difference. Now maybe Iowa people are . . . well no, I don't suppose they're any tougher than you folks or smarter. But they sure didn't spend their time arguing about the flood, or blaming someone, or waiting for anyone else to come and fix it for them. They just pulled together, got to work, and fought it. God-fearing people, just like you are here in Illinois. I suspect there's nothing they can't do when they pray and work together. I suspect that's true for all of you here tonight too."

John continued, "Look, this may not be *my* town, but I'm here now, and I like it. I want to see it survive. I'm sure willing to lend my hands to save it. I believe that if we listen to what Mr. Mosely has to say, then put our hearts and hands into it, we can do a whole lot better than what we've been doing. When we work together, we're stronger. You know the old maxim of, 'United we stand . . .'"

Raymond broke in. "The man said it right. Some flooding is coming, we know that for a fact. How much is anyone's guess. What we do know though, is that it's going to take a whole bunch of people to put an awful lot of sandbags along the creek. I'm just wondering if we're going to work together to do the right thing here, or if we're going to stand around arguing all night? Or maybe we'll hide from it and hope someone else will do the work."

Those who liked to rationalize and blame wouldn't let it go that easily. "We wouldn't have to do all this scrambling around if those in charge had done their jobs right in the first place," said one of them in the front row. Immediately, voices began bickering again from all corners of the room. Dave Mosely shrugged, and began gathering his papers together and stuffing them back into his briefcase. There was nothing more he could say.

The meeting broke up shortly after that. Raymond walked up as Linda was talking with John. Mike had just stepped out the door behind them, starting the somewhat laborious walk back to the motel.

Raymond held out his hand to John. "I'm Raymond Floyde, undersheriff of Randolph County. I appreciated your words."

John took Raymond's hand in a firm grip. "I'm John. I just said what most of the rest were thinking. Most folks will do whatever it takes to hold it together, if they're asked. These are good people. They're just scared, and sometimes scared folks freeze up and blame others instead of doing something themselves. It's hard sometimes to break them out of that long enough for them to see that there *is* a way to save themselves."

Raymond nodded."You got that right." He looked at John appraisingly. "So, how long have you been in town? Despite what you said about being a drifter, you don't talk much like one."

"This is our new hired man," explained Linda, but suddenly stopped as a wave of nausea came over her. She gripped the back of a nearby chair until her knuckles turned white, breathing deeply, hoping it would pass. Scooter saw the uneasiness in his mother's face, and slipped his hand over hers. Swallowing, she continued. "He just started today, and has already made himself irreplaceable," Linda added lightly, trying to appear as normal as possible.

Raymond noticed Linda's discomfort. She had suddenly paled, and a fine sheen of sweat broke out on her forehead. She seemed ill, but unwilling to acknowledge it. He wondered about it, then decided not to mention anything. "I'd like to stop by and talk to you about what you saw in Iowa, sometime tomorrow, if Linda can spare you for a few minutes," he said, turning back to John.

John smiled. "I'd be happy to tell you what I know, sir, but I won't be here tomorrow. Got an errand to run. I'll be back at the motel the day after tomorrow. Or maybe in the café if Charlene shanghais me to work for her." John's eyes twinkled in amusement.

Linda's stomach settled, enough for her to laugh along with Raymond at the joke. "Too bad we couldn't just get Charlene to order the river not to flood around here. It might work," she added.

Everyone chuckled. Only Scooter wasn't laughing.

# chapter 6

Shortly after midnight on Monday, 2 August 1993, just two days after John came to Hampton Corner, the levee at Valmeyer broke. The morning before it broke, John told Mike and Linda that he would be back in a day or so, and then headed up the river road to help out at Valmeyer.

Dave Mosely was there, working at a frantic pace, seemingly everywhere at once. As John worked stacking more sandbags on the levee, he wondered how Mosely could keep it up. The engineer had been running for so many long days now, stopping only briefly to sleep, grabbing food on the run. It showed too. His cheeks were hollow, his eyes sunken and frenzied.

John stretched out an arm and grabbed Dave's shoulder as he was hurrying by, calling out more orders to a group of guardsmen frantically stacking sandbags nearby. "Dave, take it easy. We're all in this together you know. Having you drop dead from exhaustion isn't going to help anybody."

Dave turned and stood winded, exhaustion written across his body. "Maybe, but I've gotta keep moving. This baby could go any second. If we don't hustle we'll lose her, and I don't think I can live with that."

John looked, and Dave followed his gaze. There was an army of National Guardsmen, local residents, state workers, and a variety of other helpers all pouring their energies into saving the levee. Reaching out again, John gently laid his hand on Dave's arm. Quietly he said, "We're all with you, buddy. We're doing all we can. All *anybody* can. If it goes, it goes. It won't be from lack of trying from anyone, certainly not you. You've done more than your best. And if it does go, we'll still need *you.*"

Dave looked into John's eyes, and saw a genuine concern that seemed to reach inside him. Suddenly he felt a wave of calm wash over him; he wasn't quite so tired, quite so frantic. His shoulders relaxed. He grinned crookedly at John. "Yeah. Okay. Thanks." And straightening his back, his step a little less burdened, his face a bit less grim, he set off again. They worked all through the night, but in the end it didn't matter.

Slowly, the water began to break through, first in a trickle, then faster in a spout, until the river burst through the levee, roaring as it came on like a freight train. The waves that tore through the crumbling levee walls were five feet high and reminded John of the white-water rapids he'd seen on the Colorado River.

Standing on the levee as the edge of it disintegrated, John grabbed Dave by the shoulders, throwing himself and Dave to safety as the part of the levee they had been standing on gave way. Lying on the wet, muddy ground, Dave tried not to cry. He groaned softly, watching the water eating away the dirt. He struggled into a sitting position and put his head on his knees.

"We're licked, it's won," said Dave, so weary that John could barely hear him over the water's roar. "You know, you always figure hard work and guts will take care of everything. If we just work hard enough, fast enough . . . well, it beat us. This river is a monster! We just couldn't catch up to it. It was like trying to grab the wind."

John could feel the engineer's despair, born of too many days trying to fight a losing battle, and his heart went out to him. "You did your best. More than that, you did the best *anyone* could. You're a good man, Dave, and a good engineer, one of the best. There was nothing more you could've done."

Dave couldn't bear the consolation right then. "You know, I've been here with all these people, and they're the greatest. I mean, we've been working night and day. We never thought the levee was going to fail. I really thought we could pull it off." He couldn't keep the tears back any longer, and wept miserably, his head in his hands.

John put his hand on Dave's shoulder as he sobbed, comforting him as best he could. He knew in his heart that sometimes there was simply no comfort man could give. But at least God could give him time and the knowledge that another soul was nearby.

When Dave finally pulled himself back together, he shook his head, seeing all over again the torrent of yellow-brown water pouring through the breach in the levee. He watched it go by, just a few feet away yet knowing he could do nothing. "It's going to cover this town in a few hours. A lot of folks have already left, but what's going to happen to those still here? There are more than nine hundred people who live here. Or *were,* anyway. Where will they go? *Why* couldn't we stop it?"

"It was too much, Dave. Too much for anyone. But you did buy them some precious time—time to gather what they could before the river took it all. That's worth a lot to these folks."

Dave blew his nose with a handkerchief. "All this talk about the army engineers taming the Mississippi is silly. No, it's worse than silly, it's stupid! You don't tame this river. Maybe all you can do is not get in its way when it wants to move. If anything, I think all our meddling has only made things worse by making people think they're safe, when it's all only stopgap measures when you get right down to it." He laughed bitterly. "Strange talk for an engineer." John just listened, sympathy in his eyes. Right now there was nothing else he could do.

A bit later, when Dave called Raymond Floyde in Hampton Corner to warn him, John stood nearby, a silent support system.

* * *

Raymond awoke instantly, knowing what the call must be. Reaching for the bedside phone his hand trembled. A threatening flu had finally taken hold during the night. He had slept poorly, and wakened achy, chilled, and feverish.

"Well Dave, we'll just do what we can down here now. How soon can you get here with your crew?"

Dave Mosely could not fathom the idea of yet another battle with the river. Exhausted, he was still trying to grasp what had happened, and he found himself rambling as he talked. "All the plans people made. All the work and ideas they had put into saving their homes, their lives from trouble. It's all worthless. You can't live like that. Life will kick you right in the teeth. It will prove all your walls don't mean anything, except to lull you into thinking you're safe, even when you aren't. Tell 'em to pack up as quick as they can and get out! It's not gonna matter what we do."

Raymond wished he were a psychologist right then, with words that could comfort his new friend. After a pause, he repeated quietly, "Dave, when will you get down here? We need you here now. "

A longer pause, then an answer. "Those creek flood walls won't hold it back. We both know that," Dave said tiredly.

"We have to try. These people here need to try."

"Even if it doesn't work?"

"Yes."

The engineer was coming back to himself, starting to think about the logistics of one more battle with the river. "I just hope we can find some more sandbags. The supply was thin up here. I'll get there as soon as I can. I'll bring whoever and whatever I can with me."

After Raymond finished the call, Jane sat up and put her arm around him. "Real bad news, huh?"

"The levee at Valmeyer gave way. That means we have two days until the water runs down the river valley and hits that little flood wall along Hampton Creek. That's real small protection against that much water."

Jane rubbed her eyes. "Is there any way to build up those creek walls enough to stop the river?"

"I don't see how. Some around here will say we can, but more will probably just pack up and run. I think the best we can do is hold it off long enough to buy us some time, or maybe slow it down a bit in the long run." Raymond stood and began to dress in his uniform. "I better call the sheriff."

Jane nodded and pulled on her robe. "I'll make you some food to take with you. I don't suppose you'll have time to get back here for a while."

"Nope."

She felt his hot forehead, and kissed him tenderly as he buttoned his shirt. "Call when you can, just so we know you're all right. And please take something for your fever before you go."

Raymond nodded and took Jane into his arms to hold her close. "Remember what we talked about? Make sure you have the seventy-two hour survival kit in the trunk of the car, pack up the most precious things, and keep what you need most close at hand."

Jane pulled back to look at him. "We have two days, don't we?"

He shrugged, then sighed. "More or less. That will go by so fast we won't believe it. And just in case, I'd rather be ready too early than too late."

She took his hand, and together they knelt beside the bed to pray.

\* \* \*

It was before the usual opening time that Monday morning, but Charlene had been unable to sleep and had gone in to open up early. She had switched on the TV at the Starbright Café to see what the latest report on the river was, and the regular customers, seeing the lights on, had already begun gathering. Charlene was leaning back against the counter, her eyes glued to the set, just like everyone else's there.

"The Mississippi," continued the newswoman, "apparently has struck its worst blow to St. Louis and rolled on. The waters have battered St. Louis since Friday, flooding hundreds of homes in suburban Chesterfield and St. Charles, forcing thousands of people to evacuate, and inundating nearby farmland. But despite continued levee breaks and lingering fears, it appears the Flood of '93 could be reaching its conclusion here after claiming forty-five lives and causing at least ten billion dollars in damage."

"Now it's our turn," said Charlene. An elderly white-haired man behind her closed his eyes and shook his head.

The newswoman continued, "Today flood waters struck the farming community of Valmeyer, Illinois, population nine hundred. Reports confirm the town is almost completely submerged. Authorities said the water gushing through a levee break last night would eventually flow unimpeded across the twenty miles of low-lying farmland to the historic town of Hampton Corner."

John sat at the counter to the left of the elderly man. No one there knew where he'd been the night before, so no one questioned how he could have gotten back so quickly. From time to time he turned to look at those in the café, and the anxiety and concern in their hearts was written clearly on their faces.

"Can I have another sweet roll?" he asked quietly. Charlene grabbed one from underneath the glass case and handed it to him without taking her eyes off the TV. John wasn't paying much attention to the news program; instead he continued to watch the people around him. In their faces he mostly saw fear building toward despair and anger. But he also saw courage and resolve.

"St. Louis took a battering this weekend," continued the newswoman, "but this Monday the Mississippi did not reach the staggering level that had been predicted. The crest, as it turned out, occurred Sunday without anyone knowing, when the river reached a record 49.4 feet; therefore, it missed the crest of the Missouri, which rolled in right on schedule this morning.

"The Mississippi dropped overnight to 48.6 feet—a level higher than many had once considered possible, but still well below the forecasted 49.7 feet. So far today no new areas in the metropolitan area are taking on water, although authorities evacuated about eight thousand people overnight in south St. Louis along the River Des Peres because of fears that fifty-one propane tanks bobbing dangerously in the swollen waters would explode.

"Even if all remains quiet, St. Louis residents will need time to put this flood into some perspective. The damage has been too great, the unknowns too many."

The TV now showed a woman who had lost her home to the flooding in the northern part of St. Louis. She was crying, without concern for what she looked like, as the newsperson asked her questions. Behind her was a large area of water where several homes lay submerged almost to the top of their first-floor windows.

"We've lost *everything*," wailed the woman, "everything we had. The river took it all. My husband has been out of work for months and now, I don't know what we'll do. It's just too much!"

Linda walked in the door behind the café counter, shaking her head as she saw the scene between the distraught woman and the newsperson. "Why can't they leave the poor woman alone? Isn't it bad enough that she's suffered such loss? Why do they insist on exploiting her pain like that?"

John tapped the counter, thinking. "A lot of people have traveled to the Midwest to help because they saw something like that on the news. It's made people more aware of their neighbors and of how precious life is. So maybe some good can come out of a story like that."

Linda turned to study him, a little surprised at his words.

"And I also agree with you," he added, "some of it goes too far."

Charlene turned and smiled at John. "You need some more orange juice, hon?"

Linda had to bite her lip to keep from snickering at Charlene. Charlene had been married and divorced five times, but fondly remembered every one of them. Was she hoping for number six? Quickly, to distract herself from the thought, Linda picked up a clean cup and poured some hot water from the glass kettle. In a moment she had an herbal tea bag steeping in the cup. "You picked a strange time to come to town," she said to John.

"Oh, I don't know," he answered, taking the new glass of juice from Charlene. "Looks like before the day is through we're going to need all the hands we can get for those sandbags. Maybe I picked the best time to be here."

"Forty-seven thousand acres in the valley," said the old man at the counter next to him. "The best farmland in the world, and it's all going to be buried under Mississippi mud."

Charlene turned to look. "You sold your farm three months ago, didn't you, Henry?"

Henry nodded gravely. "My grandson is working it now. He's the fourth generation of our family to work that land. Promised he'd do it right, he did. Now it's all for nothing. After all these years, the darn river is going to take it all."

John would have liked to say there was a way to save the farm, but there wasn't. No power on earth could save the farms between Valmeyer and Hampton Corner. And the town was in danger too.

"I'm sorry," said John, touching the man's arm.

"Me too young fellow, but it don't change anything."

There was more TV news about the flooding, much of it a repeat of what they had seen earlier. John finished his breakfast and excused himself. Going out the back door, he felt a prompting and followed it around behind the main motel building. He found Mike scooping up and smelling handfuls of mud.

"Looks like the river is moving in," said John.

Caught off guard, Mike turned, teetering on his crutches. He regarded John suspiciously before saying, "This is just between me and you. I don't want my wife to know. All she'll do is worry about it."

"But don't you think Linda is tough enough to face the facts?"

Mike nodded, but his words said otherwise. "She wouldn't want to know that her aunt left her a run-down motel that probably won't ever be worth much. This is the first thing that's truly belonged to her and it means more to her than you can understand. And on top of all that, it's built on land too close to the river." Mike clumsily reached down and picked up another handful of mud. "It's always wet back here. But now it's worse. The higher the river gets, the worse the mud gets." Mike shook his head angrily. "Seems like some sick kind of cosmic connection, don't it?"

John looked up at the sky. "Then why are you so determined to save this place? Why not just give up, Mike?"

Mike tossed the mud aside and wiped off his hands. "Because I've never had anything and neither has Linda. Because I'm tired of being a nobody. Because—" He stopped, frustrated, and shrugged.

"Because it's the right thing to do," John finished for him. He picked up a stone and threw it over the levee. The men could just hear a faint plop in the river behind the dirt mound. "Because not trying, not fighting for something better, is like laying down and dying."

Mike's eyes widened at John's words, which were almost exactly what a priest in Mexico had once told the little Miguel. Bruised and beaten, the small child was cleaned up and cared for by the young priest, so different from the old ones who cursed him.

"Always remember," the young priest had said, "it is better to fall down from trying to be something better, than to lie down and give up. When you give up, it's all over. You die." Mike had never forgotten the man, or his words.

And now here was this John, saying those very words to him in this unlikely place. Mike felt a momentary urge to trust John, to pour out all his fears and concerns to this man who felt like a friend. But the influence of his difficult upbringing was stronger than all his new changes in life. A wall of silence filled the space between the two men, a world of differences. Mike was sure no one could understand how different those worlds were. Certainly not this gringo, kind eyes or not. What would he know about that kind of pain, that kind of desperation?

As if reading Mike's thoughts, John shrugged and turned away. "I'll get the shovels ready," he said, walking toward the storage shed, then added, "I imagine the sandbag army will be gathering today."

John stopped and looked back, right into Mike's worried brown eyes. "Mike, remember, you're not alone in this. People care. *God* cares. Something good will come of all this, Mike, even if we can't save the motel. Keep your heart open to new horizons, Mike, and don't give up."

Mike watched John walk off, then looked up at the top of the levee, feeling a burning in his heart, but not sure why. John seemed to have the same confidence Linda did in God, maybe more. And it seemed to give him extra peace—extra resolve. Mike felt that extra resolve well up in him. He was tired of running, tired of losing. Maybe now was the time he would find out once and for all if he was tough enough to take the beating and stay on his feet. If he was strong enough to win the battle. And he wanted so badly to win.

# chapter 7

Daybreak found Raymond trying to get a feel for the flood water as it gobbled up the Tillman River Valley. He drove slowly along the little two-lane highway that ran above the river along the foothills east of the valley. Down below he could see many bizarre items being carried along in the water. Some of them were gruesome. At one point he came around a bend and was horrified to find caskets bobbing along in the flood waters. They had been flushed out of the Valmeyer Cemetery and were now eerily weaving through the other debris in the crowded waters, making their way south toward Hampton Corner. It really got to him, and he felt sick for quite a while after.

Finally, he pulled his patrol car over and stood on a hill overlooking Valmeyer. Five miles out of town he saw an abandoned trailer. He assumed the rig had become stuck in a ditch on a nearby road, and the driver, seeing the river coming, must have unhitched his load and driven off in the cab. As Raymond watched, the trailer lurched in the flood waters, tilted to one side, and then slid slowly into the muddy mess, disappearing into the yellow-brown river.

Technically he wasn't responsible for anything here, as he worked for Randolph County, which just barely extended five miles north of Hampton Corner. But how could he ignore a town needing help? He couldn't, which was why he found himself helping a farmer move a herd of frightened, wet cows into a small country church that sat on a raised knoll, leaving them to huddle miserably together in the unusual makeshift shelter until they could be rescued. Strange times made for strange solutions.

Raymond started out again. Near eleven o'clock he was driving south down the narrow country road that linked Valmeyer and Hampton Corner. The road was still above water for now, but it wouldn't be for long. Soon, everything in the valley would be covered with roiling yellow-brown river water. At one point he stopped and watched the flood line eat up corn fields.

As one Valmeyer resident had said, "It's just a *leisurely* disaster. You know it's coming, and there isn't anything you can do about it. Except possibly get out of the way!"

For those last few moments, if you didn't look too close at the Tillman River Valley, it appeared that farm life was going on just like it always had for so many years. Everything still felt so peaceful and secure. The quiet rural farm life had not changed much since the 1700s. People had given their all eking out a hard-won life here, making it a place where their families could live and love and hope and dream. It was hard to believe it was only hours away from changing forever. Turning his patrol car back toward Hampton Corner, Raymond tried to turn his thoughts away from the despair that threatened to overwhelm him. *Trust in God, Raymond,* he told himself sternly. *Trust in God. Where one door closes, another opens.*

Raymond uttered a silent prayer on his way to a meeting. Herman Mombow, the president of Tillman River Valley Levee District, had called an emergency gathering of the district officers, and dispatch had notified Raymond. He would be there, representing the sheriff's office, particularly since Sheriff Picou was flat on his back with the worst migraine of his life. Picou's words on the phone to Raymond had been very clear.

"Think of this, Floyde," said Picou, his voice soft with pain, but strained in intensity. "With me down, it's all in your lap. But if you screw up, and let those knotheads along the river make things worse, the commissioners will come after *me.* That's the way the job works. And know this, if I hang, *you'll* go with me."

The phone line had gone dead as Pete hung up, leaving Raymond feeling like he'd been punched in the face. Raymond rolled his eyes. His own head hadn't felt too good before that, and now it was worse. The flu continued to haunt him, and he was still struggling with the occasional wave of nausea too. *Great. The biggest disaster this area has ever known and both the sheriff and I are sick.* Raymond prayed fervently to be healed, and inspired.

Dave Mosely had talked with him on the radio a few hours before about busting a hole in the levee to try to divert the worst of the flood into the valley—which would change the water pressure against the town's flood walls—and at least save the town. But would the Army Corps of Engineers agree to that, as well as the farmers in the Levee District? Farmers were a stubborn and smart bunch. Purposely flooding their land would not be an easy sell. But if they could be convinced this was a kind of solution, they would go for it. The question was, *would* it work?

If punching a hole longer than a football field in the river levee didn't make any difference, and Hampton Corner flooded anyway, Raymond knew he could start looking for another job, in another part of the country. There would be many angry people looking to blame someone, even if they would have been flooded out anyway. And Randolph County was still controlled by the farmers, who, when they finally did come together to make their desires known, fought until they got what they wanted.

\* \* \*

John was walking along the river road between Hampton Corner and Valmeyer. He was just taking his time, almost as if he expected someone to come along anytime and pick him up. In fact, he did expect someone.

He had done a lot of walking through the years. Had spent more time alone than with people. As a precocious teenager, he had told his mother, "I wish I could just have some time to myself." John grinned. *Need to remember to be careful what I wish for!*

A raven flew by overhead, banked left, circled around, and finally came to light just to one side of John. The two of them were a sight, walking down the road together.

"Hey, Mr. Raven. If you're looking for a handout, you're knocking on the wrong door today."

The bird kept walking, but cocked its head to one side looking the man over. Then it squawked once, paused, then again.

"Okay, so you just want to talk. I can do that. So, flood kind of cut into your business?"

The bird nodded, and John laughed at the coincidence.

"Have you been to the MacFarland place today?"

The Raven squawked three times.

"Yeah, I imagine they're going to have to get out pretty quick."

The bird stopped and tilted its head to listen down the road toward the north. Then without any more squawking it took off. John watched it fly away.

A half minute later, Raymond Floyde came up behind him in his patrol car, moving south, and came to a stop.

There was a surprised look on Raymond's face. "What're you doing out here in the middle of nowhere?"

John smiled, and without an invitation jumped into the deputy's car. "Just out for a stroll, looking around. Thought I would see who might need some help getting ready for the flooding. Looks like that's what you're doing too. Okay if I join you?"

Raymond nodded, feeling that something wasn't right, but not sure what. It just seemed strange this guy would be out here wandering by himself at a time like this. But then, this guy *was* different, in ways Raymond could feel but not explain. There was something about him . . . not a *bad* something; on the contrary, this something made you want to trust this stranger. It wasn't a feeling Raymond usually had about folks, and it made him nervous. He eyed John warily, and John grinned innocently back at him.

Raymond cleared his throat and coughed a bit. "Okay. I guess so. Sure. I mean, we can always use a spare hand at a time like this." As he said it, he knew it was true, but wondered what it was about this John that made him so nervous. What in the name of heaven *was* he doing out here in the middle of nowhere?

* * *

As Raymond turned into Jeff MacFarland's corn and pig farm, he found himself once more thinking how beautiful it was. City people wouldn't have appreciated how gorgeous a pig farm was, but coming from a farm in Nebraska himself, he did. At times like this he wondered why he wasn't still there, back on the farm he had known and loved for most of his life.

The MacFarland twins roared past the car out the driveway, riding together on the tractor and towing a large, loaded flatbed trailer behind them. They waved and yelled enthusiastically as they passed, and John waved back at them. The farm evacuations had begun.

In front of the house were parked five pickup trucks alongside the cream-colored station wagon with a produce logo on its side. Raymond recognized it as the mayor's car. Hampton Corner's mayor, Bill Smooty, owned the town grocery store.

"If you want to wait a bit, I'll give you a ride back into town after we finish up here at this meeting," Raymond told John as he climbed out of the patrol car. John nodded in acknowledgment. As Raymond got out of his car, Jenine Gorblancher, county commissioner for that part of the county, pulled in behind him. She got out of her green Jeep Wrangler and they nodded at each other. "Guess this is the place," she said. "How's things looking up toward Valmeyer?" John smiled at her. She saw it, but didn't return it. She just stared at him for a moment and then turned her attention back to Raymond.

"Town's all evacuated, and the water is making good time on its way here," answered Raymond. "The valley is going under as we speak, and it won't be too long before we're feeling it here. We haven't got much time to waste, that's for sure."

Jeff MacFarland appeared in the back doorway of the farmhouse, and waved at them to come in. "Let's go, time's a wasting," muttered Jenine, and she headed into the house.

"Who's your friend? Catch an early looter, did you?" asked Jeff, looking past Raymond's shoulder toward the patrol car where John now lounged against the door.

"Just someone looking to help out," replied Raymond. "We can always use another hand."

\* \* \*

Jeff MacFarland drew boxes on the notepad in front of him— boxes linked together, boxes stacked on top of each other. The conversation droned on around him. Tiring of it, he laid the pencil down and said, "So, what you're saying . . ."

Herman Mombow's last words were interrupted by Jeff. The old farmer frowned, but let the young pup take center stage

". . . is we can't rebuild the flood wall on the creek's north, protecting us here in the valley. Okay. That's obvious. And the flood waters are coming no matter what we do. Also obvious. And you say the only thing that will preserve the creek's south flood wall, and save the town, is to bust a four-hundred-foot hole in the river levee down this way, and let the two currents meet. But what I don't get is how putting *more* water into the valley is going to keep the town from going under. Shouldn't we just—"

Jenine Gorblancher jumped in. "The water pressure forces the flow to either go out the hole we make for it, or jump the southern flood wall and break out a hole some place just south of Hampton corner—after washing out the town."

"I know, Jenine, I understand *that.*" Jeff's sarcasm was obvious. He hadn't liked Jenine ever since they were in high school. She was a senior when he was a freshman, and she had never let him forget that he was a just another farm boy and she was the daughter of a wealthy doctor. All these years later her actions still rankled him. "How," he continued with his original question, "do we know the creek's southern flood walls can't be built up enough to stop the water? Why go looking for more trouble?"

"That creek flood wall *will* have to be built up, no matter what else we do, in an effort to control the direction of the flow," put in Raymond. "Dave Muller and the National Guard units have already begun coordinating the effort along the creek."

"The farmers aren't going to like this," said Herman. "You don't knock down levees in flood time. You put them up."

"Yeah, so what do you want from us?" piped in another member of the district board. "Clearly this is not what we want to do, but it sounds like we have to, or *nothing* will survive around here. It's pretty much a done deal, isn't that what you're saying?" He turned back to Raymond.

Raymond nodded. "We have to be willing to give up something to save something. That's just how it is. And we're going to be darn lucky if we manage to save anything anyhow."

Mayor Smooty held out his hands on the big round kitchen table, a silent plea to the men he faced. "We need your help with the creek flood wall. We have to raise it up much higher than it is now. The National Guard will help, but they aren't enough. We need you, and we need your equipment. Besides, we all have a stake in the town, even those of you who live out here in the valley. Now is the time we really need to pull together."

"Geez, you don't want much," said Jeff. "You're asking *us* to let *our* whole lives, *our* homes, be washed out by a man-made flood, and then come help the townspeople save *their* places? How many of *them* are out there on the sandbag line? I'll bet a lot of them have just up and left. Besides, we all still have animals and equipment to get out of the valley."

"We'll get a good share of the town folk to come and help" the mayor insisted. "You won't be doing this alone. You'll see."

Jeff muttered a swear word, then began drawing boxes again, only this time they were bobbing on a river.

Herman Mombow looked around the table. "Okay. I think the mayor has laid out a pretty clear picture for us. Doesn't look like we have too much choice, if we want to save anything, and I think we all agree that we do want to save what we can. What do you say? Are we in agreement that the levee needs a hole in it, and we just need to decide where?" No answers, just a few nods. "Anyone know how to do that exactly? I mean, how to put the hole in it when it's already full of water and all?"

"Maybe you pull it down just the opposite of how you put it up," sniped Jenine.

Jeff smiled, thinking how little she had learned, or changed, over the years. Still the same ol' uppity Jenine.

Raymond had a thought. "Where can we get a barge crane with a bucket on it?"

"I have an idea where we just might do that," said Jenine, her sarcasm gone. Jeff was caught off guard, then found himself smiling even bigger. So maybe she wasn't the *exact* same ol' uppity Jenine.

* * *

John, meanwhile, was enjoying the MacFarland farm and the MacFarlands. The twins were back, and laughing at a story he was telling them while they all loaded up the flatbed for their next trip.

". . . so the farmer," continued John, "sold the tractor to his neighbor, but then it started right up. Without any trouble at all."

The boys doubled up with laughter at how the dishonest farmer got it in the end. "You couldn't pull that on Dad, but he'd think it was funny if it happened to someone else."

Natalie came out of the house, saw her brothers with John, and stopped to watch them.

"Natalie?" called John, waving her over. "Come sit with us."

The girl frowned, and went back into the house. "Mom?" she called up the stairs. "Mom?"

Sandy popped her head out of the bedroom. "What?"

"Who's that out front with the twins?"

Sandy went over to her bedroom window and peered out. First she frowned, then her eyes grew wide. "Oh my heavens! It's not—why, he doesn't look a day over—it is! It's John!" In a flash, she tore out of the bedroom, down the stairs, and past a bewildered Natalie.

"Mom?"

When Natalie came out, she found her mother hugging the stranger like he was her long-lost brother. Laughing, Sandy stepped back out of the man's arms a moment, and then hugged him again. "What are you doing here?" she asked. "It's been years and miles and—" but then interrupted herself with, "Natalie, honey, come here. I want you to meet John."

* * *

Half an hour later the meeting inside the house broke up. Raymond was last to leave, talking with Jeff as they came out the back door onto the large porch. Jeff was still complaining about how the farmers were expected to save the town, and risk their equipment, when not one townie in a hundred would do the same for them.

"Aren't you always saying farmers are better than city folk? Here's your chance to prove it." Raymond prodded.

The words passed right over Jeff. He was staring across the farmyard at Sandy. She was coming across the yard, passing under the oak trees. A man walked next to her, her arm linked with his as they walked toward the house, Sandy talking animatedly. The stranger seemed way too comfortable holding onto Sandy, *way* too familiar for Jeff's liking.

Raymond, recognizing John, stared. "Well, I'll be! Reckon he knew where he was headed after all," he muttered under his breath, eyeing Jeff carefully.

"What was that?" Jeff asked Raymond, staring hard at Sandy.

"Nothing. Nothing at all. I'll be heading out of here now, Jeff. Got lots to do." Raymond stepped off the porch and walked quickly to his car. Jeff nodded absently in Raymond's direction, his eyes still pinned on Sandy and the stranger as they approached the house.

Sandy waved with her free hand. "Jeff, come here. I want you to meet someone." Natalie followed a distance behind the two, her sharp eyes missing nothing about this most interesting situation.

"This is John, he helped me . . ." Sandy could not quite find the words. Finally, raising her eyes to meet Jeff's she blurted, "When Adam was dying, it was John who got me through it all."

Jeff eyed the stranger even more intensely. "That right? You a doctor?"

John shook his head and smiled. "I was an orderly in the hospital where Adam died." He held out his hand to Jeff and tried to meet Jeff's eyes. But Jeff looked away and left John holding his hand out to nothing, pretending he didn't see it. Sandy didn't notice, or didn't act as if she did. She was bubbling over with excitement, which bothered Jeff.

"John's the best man with a wheelchair or gurney I ever saw. Pure art to behold." Sandy giggled, practically beaming. "John, come on in. We'll find you something to take the edge off your hunger. Do you still like grilled cheese sandwiches?"

"Sandy! We don't have time for this," Jeff said to her as she and John went past him into the house. "We need to get busy clearing out of here."

Waving off Jeff's concerns, Sandy called back to him, "It'll only take a few moments, Jeff. We'll be okay. We've all got to eat anyway, don't we?" All eyes and ears, the children ghosted into the house behind them.

Jeff stared at their backs as they stepped through the open screen door. Now alone in the barnyard, he decided not to go back inside the house. He could hear Sandy's happy chatter and John's slow, deep laughter. Jeff walked up on the porch. He was suddenly so angry he felt like breaking something. Who *was* this guy? And more importantly, who was he to Sandy?

* * *

"Cob, are you out of your mind?" Mayor Smooty couldn't believe his ears. "You're really *not* going to haul sand for the bagging?"

Cob Kortland was a rotund little man with large arms. At the moment, he was clasping his large belly, while shaking his head emphatically. "I already told you, I have a contract with the state that takes up all my trucks. I can't do a thing for you, Mayor. That's just the way it is."

"But you *live* here in Hampton. If we can't keep the water back, your home will be flooded just like the rest."

"My ten dump trucks are more important than my house. I can always get another house, but my trucks are my bread and butter. Besides, you can get someone else to haul for you. How about your farmer buddies?"

Mayor Smooty suddenly decided why this man had never married. He was great at what he did, but stubborn and shortsighted. "Your trucks are designed for this kind of hauling; anything else won't work as well, and you know it. It'll take us two or three times as long trying to haul sand in trucks that weren't built for it. We just don't have the time." Frustrated, Smooty pled, "Cob, we can't do this without you."

"Oh, I reckon you could find enough pickup trucks and such around here if'n you really wanted to. But it sure seems like folks don't wanna help save their own town, don't it?" Cob watched the mayor slyly out of the corner of his eye.

Smooty tapped his leg impatiently. "Don't you suppose the state would appreciate you helping out the community? They might even lengthen your contract with them because of it."

The little trucker leaned over to spit a wad of chewing tobacco. "Mayor, there ain't a thing you can give me I can't get for myself. You don't know half the people I know."

Smooty winced, but would not be denied and came down hard. "I'd hate to have to have the trucks seized by the county for the duration of the emergency."

Cob snorted. "Try it. Besides, it'll take you too long to do it legally. Or are you saying you'll point a gun at me and take away what's mine? I've worked hard for what I got, and it's mine to say what I do with it! You try anything illegal, and just maybe it'll all blow up in your face!"

"It's not going to kill you to help out here. What's your problem?"

The truck owner kept silent, his small eyes narrowing.

Smooty threw up his hands and walked off, slamming the door behind him and muttering to himself. What was wrong with people? Couldn't they see past the end of their noses?

# chapter 8

Now that John had eaten and had gone to help the twins with their work, Sandy looked over her list for the hundredth time in the last hour. Forgetting to remove anything important from their home could have disastrous long-term consequences. The flood would spare nothing.

Much of the hog and chicken feed was already gone, stashed in the barn of a friend who fortunately occupied a place up on the hills to the east. The chickens would not be too much trouble to round up, but the pigs would. So when John and the twins got back from driving and hauling the farm tools, the pigs would be next out. Jeff, meanwhile, was in and out of the house helping Sandy and Natalie with the first floor of the house.

Everything had to go.

Natalie was going back and forth through the house carrying armloads of clothes, dumping them into the back of one of their pickup trucks. There was no time to be compulsive about cleanliness and order—that could be taken care of later. Jeff had stacked some of their mattresses on the back porch to take along in case they were needed. A friend of Sandy's who lived on high ground in Hampton Corner had offered them a place to stay.

Jeff came back into the kitchen, looked around, and angrily ripped the phone off the wall. Then he looked sadly into the family room at his beloved pool table. Its thick slate tabletop made it too heavy to waste time on. Shaking his head he knocked the back screen door out of the way with an elbow and left the house.

Sandy reflected on Jeff's moods. They used to make her mad, those first few years they were married, and they had had their share of fights over them. Pretty pointless, she had finally realized; getting mad at a man for getting mad. Now her heart just ached for him. Why was the man so self-destructively stubborn? And what on earth had him going now? She took a deep breath and, vowing again not to let him get to her, let it out slowly. Then she got back to work.

At that moment John and the twins came roaring into the farm compound, truck radio blaring. The boys' eyes were sparkling. Obviously this was great fun for them. It gave them a break from routine and a chance for some adventure. In their short-sighted and youthful way, they hoped the emergency would last a long time. John rode in the truck bed, seeming completely calm. Sandy grinned, watching them. She couldn't be too downhearted with such buoyant and positive personalities around. She was still stunned to find John here, but Lord knew they needed someone like him at a time like this!

"I'm out of here!" hollered Jeff from outside the house.

Sandy yelled back, "Okay!" She didn't really need Jeff's help cleaning out the house, but it was nice to have him around, even if he was an old grump right now. Suddenly she was afraid. Afraid of what the flood meant for their future. When it all settled down, then she could really worry. But for now, it was full steam ahead—survival required action, not reflection.

Natalie took the last load of clothes out to the truck and came back into the kitchen. "Do we want to take the pictures off the walls?"

Sandy nodded. "Yeah. Put them upstairs in your room, sweetie. The water probably won't reach the second floor, at least, I hope not." Before Natalie could move, Sandy caught herself. "Except for your Aunt Myrna's painting. That seascape is the only original artwork in this whole house, except for what you kids have made for me. I don't want anything to happen to it, so bring it on down and load it up."

"Gotcha," answered Natalie.

Stacking the wall pictures in a pile in the middle of the living room, Natalie paused. "Mom?"

Sandy pulled her head out from under the kitchen sink where she was kneeling. Each hand held a can of cleaning solution. "Yeah?"

"Will the house still be here when the water goes away?"

Sandy stopped short, uncertain how to answer. How could she answer? She had no idea what was going to happen. When she heard no answer, Natalie came back to stand in the doorway between the kitchen and living room. While this was home to all of them, for Natalie it was the only home she had ever known.

"I . . . want to say it will." Sandy looked up into her daughter's eyes and saw how far that fell short of comforting her. "I don't know, baby. I guess it depends on how deep the water gets and how fast the current is. This old house is pretty strong—the foundation is solid. I think it'll be okay. Your dad would know more about that than I do."

Natalie shrugged halfheartedly and went back into the living room. Sandy rose from the floor and set the cleaning bottles in a large box on the big kitchen table. Her eyes traveled around the room, going over how she had changed the place, making it hers. She had left some of what Jeff's mother had, but gotten rid of almost all of what Kathy had done. Other than loving Jeff, it appeared Sandy and Kathy had very little in common.

So what *was* going to happen to the place?

Sandy had no previous experience with such a calamity. There had been frequent earthquakes in California, even a few strong ones as she was growing up. But those were over and done with in moments, leaving whatever damage had been done. There was not much chance to prepare or to prevent it; it just *was*. A flood was a slow-motion disaster. You knew it was coming, could make some plans, take some precautions, but there was still the unknown of what the damage would be.

Something caught her eye near the back door. Curious, she went over and picked up the smooth, plastic casing that held Natalie's leaf. It felt good in Sandy's hand. Suddenly all her worries came together in a lump in her stomach: quick tears wet her eyes, and she bit her lip, trying to hold it all back. "Oh, Lord!" she said softly, remembering Robbie, feeling again his loss, and realizing they might lose the house—the house that still held so much of Robbie in it. She brushed at her eyes with the back of her sleeve.

*Life is never what you thought it was going to be. Plans never work out exactly like you want them to. And if you dwell too long on the disappointments, they will crush you. Better to go on, keep moving, don't think about them too much, don't dwell on them. Enjoy what is good, and give the rest to God.* Sandy rehearsed this much-used litany yet again, fighting to gain control of her emotions.

Sandy believed in God, but never was much for "organized reli-gion." She went to a small community church on occasion, but only casually. Sometimes she envied people who seemed to have such a personal relationship with a friendly, involved, caring God. She tended to think of God as someone that cared about people generally—like a monarch—not as someone who knew and cared about everyone person-ally. She couldn't imagine much beyond that, couldn't understand how a deeply personal God could watch bad things happen in this crazy world.

John had that kind of relationship with God. When he was around, she could almost feel God standing behind him. John had been the one who had somehow helped her heal her broken heart when Adam was dying. It was John's faith that had filled her heart with hope and belief. John had shown her his vision of God, and for that brief moment in time, she had felt as if she too could feel God. Sometimes since then she thought she could feel Him nearby, comforting her. Sometimes.

Right that moment she longed to be able to feel His love again, to have the comfort of heavenly arms around her.

Instead, as Natalie came through the kitchen with some pictures, Sandy reached out and grasped her only daughter in her arms. "I love you, baby. We'll get through this okay. We will. It'll all work out, and somehow we'll make it. I promise."

Suddenly, there was a loud crash behind them causing both of them to jump. Natalie had bumped the kitchen table, and the cleaning bottles fell, smashing on the floor.

"I'm sorry, Mom. I'll get it."

"Nah, I can do it. Here," she handed the plastic leaf over, "you go finish taking the pictures upstairs."

While Sandy was cleaning up the floor, a thought occurred to her. *Here I am making sure my floor is clean, and before too long, the whole river will be running through here.* She laughed at herself and kept on cleaning—*don't want anyone to slip on it*, she rationalized.

*    *    *

The trailer full of pigs that Jeff was hauling behind his tractor swung around too far and sideswiped one of the stately oak trees along the driveway. He winced, seeing the explosion of bark. Kathy would be mad about that one. Then he remembered the river was coming.

*Stupid. Why worry about a tree right now? Pretty soon everything will be going down river. My whole life is going down river.*

A moment later it hit him. *Kathy?* He had thought of *Kathy*, not Sandy. What was that all about? Kathy hadn't lived there for years. But it had been Kathy who had loved the trees so much.

Thinking of his wife sparked a brief memory of John from that afternoon, after Jeff had finally calmed down and gone in to lunch. He had watched John and tried to figure out just what his relationship to Sandy was. He'd decided maybe it was no big deal after all. Sandy was happy to see John, but maybe that was it, and John certainly wasn't overly familiar with Sandy. Besides, like Raymond had said, they could always use another hand, especially right now. And John was very willing. Liked to talk as he worked though, and Jeff liked to work in silence. No harm in that, Jeff guessed, so long as it didn't slow them down, and it didn't seem to slow John one bit.

Earlier, as the two of them loaded pigs into the trailer, John had said something like, "It's the memories you try to push away that follow you the hardest." Jeff had wondered what in the world he was talking about. He was an odd sort of guy, that John. Good with pigs though, which surprised Jeff. John, in his sandals and longish hair didn't look like a pig farmer, not any Jeff had known anyway. They'd loaded the frightened animals much faster than Jeff had thought they'd be able to. But he couldn't help wondering, though, at the glow John brought out in Sandy. It bothered him a great deal more than he wanted to admit. Sandy, attracted to a wandering nobody like John? He shook the thought from his head. Nah. But still . . . there was *something* there between the two of them.

Jeff shifted gears and prepared himself for the drive up the hill to his friend's farm. There was a shed on the property where the pigs could be put for a while.

As the tractor plowed steadily along with its load of squealing pigs, he found himself thinking about his corn crop, then crop insurance, then flood insurance. Who had flood insurance on their crops around here? Who could afford it? *The levee was supposed to be our insurance.*

*Coward*, he heard in his head. *You're running away instead of fighting.*

*So how do I fight the river?* he raged at the unseen voice.

*Here you don't*, a quieter, calmer voice spoke. *But in town they'll need you.*

Once Jeff had his own place cleared out he planned on helping his farm neighbors. But the town? Maybe when he was finished.

The country road twisted around toward the north. Before long, he could look over to the side and see his place. As the road rose higher than the river valley, Jeff caught glimpses of the sun reflecting off the flood waters that gobbled up the valley like a swarm of maddened locusts. His throat tightened. It wasn't fair. The land belonged to *him* now. He'd worked his guts out trying to make it into a paying farm, something his family could depend on. Now it was all going to be gone? Just like that?

The road twisted east and he lost his view, and the angry, frustrated voice took over again.

*Yeah, you just think it belongs to you. You think you own something. But, you don't, it's just on loan.*

He looked up at the cloudless blue. The rain was gone now, but the flood was still coming, and on a clear, beautiful day. It was downright ironic.

Riding the tractor had always given Jeff plenty of time to think. And the more he thought right then, the worse he felt. Who was to blame here? *Somebody* had to be responsible. After so many years without flooding problems, why should all this happen now?

*Grow up, man!* Jeff shook himself. Why blame anyone? Bad stuff happens, especially in farming. He knew that. Just accept things and go on.

John and the twins passed him, going the opposite way back to the farm to pick up another load of pigs. And in just a split second, before Jeff could once again be critical of them, the Spirit showed him something.

He had been so sure the twins would turn out like Kathy, so sure blood would tell in the end, that they would be no-account bums who would run out on responsibility. No matter that they were half his, no matter that Sandy had been their mother longer than Kathy had. No, Jeff had been sure that if he didn't crush every bit of Kathy in them, their lives would be worthless. But they weren't worthless. They weren't. They worked hard and did as they were told, and although they were rambunctious, they weren't in any way bad kids. Never got into any real trouble. They were good boys. They were *his* boys. And what had all his negative feelings brought him, and them? Jeff was sure that deep down, the boys loved him, but he knew they didn't like or trust him much. Why should they? When had he ever taken the time to enjoy them?

When Jeff pulled into his friend's farm, he put his thoughts away and focused on the work at hand. But after the pigs were unloaded, and he was headed back toward his own place, his thoughts came right back. The earlier revelation about the twins had set his mind on a track he'd never covered before. And though he was harsher with himself than anyone else would be, what he began thinking had some merit to it.

*If your brother hadn't ducked out, you wouldn't even be here now. This would have been* his *place. And you didn't care, remember? You only came back because there was no one else to do it. So from that moment on you wouldn't let yourself dislike any of it, for fear you would give up and run away.*

*What about Natalie? Did you take out much time to be her father? What about Robbie? He was a great kid and look at how you drove him. Drove him too hard. If it weren't for you, he'd be alive today . . .*

He shook his head trying to make the voice stop. It wouldn't.

*Your farm is never going to be the same again. You know that, and there's not a thing you can do to change it. Besides, the farm is just a thing. You pour all your blood, sweat, and tears into it, and it can't love you back. Not the way your family could, if you'd give them half of what you've given this farm. . . . And someday, if you don't get smart, you'll wake up, and be all alone. No farm, no family, no Sandy, nothing. All alone except for your pride. That's what you'll have to keep you company. And you know what? You'll deserve to be alone. You will have earned it.*

When he got back to the house, Sandy was struggling to get a dresser out the back door. Jeff jumped down off the tractor and helped her lift it into the back of the pickup.

As they finished, he touched her arm briefly and said, "I love you."

Sandy's eyebrows lifted in surprise, and she smiled. "I love you too."

He started to get back on the tractor, but guilt at not being there for her so many times tugged him back. He pulled Sandy against him in a tight hug.

Surprised, she hugged him back, but he held on, his nose buried in the soft scent of her hair. "Jeff? What's gotten into you?"

Jeff's grip loosened and he released her gently, shrugging. "I don't know." He smiled sheepishly, suddenly embarrassed, and jumped back on the tractor.

Sandy watched him drive away, wondering what he meant, and figuring his emotions were charged by the threat of the flood. Today was an emotional time for them all, she guessed. Their anniversary party had not been much fun. Jeff was moodier than usual, and she was stressed about the news of Kathy—she still hadn't even told Jeff what she knew. It had been a long, stiff evening. But that was days ago. What had gotten into the man now?

The fishing tackle box and new gear from the party still lay on the stairs where Jeff had left them days ago. Obviously Sandy had missed on that present, even though he had talked several times about wanting to get back to fishing again. She should have known. Jeff never took time off for anything or anybody. It was always drive, drive, drive. She wondered briefly if all farmers were that way. Maybe it was just her farmer.

"Mom?" came the call from out the upstairs window. "Mom?"

Sandy reluctantly let go of her thoughts and returned to her job. "Coming." She would ask Jeff later what was going on. First he was even more moody than usual, then suddenly he was hugging her. Obviously *something* was going on. But she finally shrugged it off and went into the house.

John stood back between the two small sheds, watching. From where he stood he could see Jeff driving away up the road and Sandy walking back into the house. He could see the deep emotions beginning to come alive in Jeff, and he wanted to make sure they didn't get capped over again, as they had so often in the past. The MacFarland family needed to come together, to reach out more openly to each other. The love was there, it just had to be rekindled. That love would bind them together and give them strength and synergy like nothing else could. John stood very still, his eyes not focused on anything of this world, his mind far away. Finally, he looked up at the sky, listened, smiled as he nodded, and went back to getting more pigs ready to go. He had an inspired plan. The rest was all just a matter of time.

# chapter 9

With equal parts sweat and spirit, the backbreaking work of sand-bagging began in Hampton Corner. By Monday afternoon, members of the 110-man National Guard unit that had worked on the Valmeyer levee were intermingled with the townspeople along the south side of Hampton Creek. John and Scooter were working together near the west end. While Scooter tied a sandbag shut, John paused from steadying it to look north toward Valmeyer. As the flood waters filled the valley, they would eventually cover the two-lane byway across the creek, and the smaller flood wall on the north side of the creek would overflow.

To save the town from the flood, the small flood wall on the south needed to be elevated to at least three times its current height. But that meant quickly completing a project that stretched over half a mile from the Mississippi River all the way to the higher ground on the east.

Orange dump trucks from the department of transportation busily brought load after load of sand, gravel, and rocks. Everyone was working smoothly, although with different levels of effort. All were covered in mud and filth. But there were no unhappy faces, just determined, tired, or worried ones. The project was new, and enthusiasm was high. Valmeyer might have lost, but there was still a chance Hampton Corner would survive.

So far every sandbag was full, tight to the top, since things weren't rushed yet. The time when the river would be pushing on the emergency levee—when it might take one foot to hold down a new bag from floating up until another could be piled on top of it—was still a ways off.

Scooter was sweating heavily in the bright sunlight and humid air, but his spirit was strong. "Ouch!" he yelped. As he had tried to seal off the bag in John's grasp, the rough edges of the material had cut a deep slice in his hand. He tucked his hurt hand up into his armpit, nursing it with a grimace of pain on his freckled face.

John took over and finished sealing the bag. Then reaching out to Scooter, he asked, "Can I look at it?" Scooter produced his hurt hand. John pressed the little boy's hand between his. "Let's go find a first aid kit," John said. Scooter felt his cut begin to sting sharply and tears welled up in his eyes.

As John expertly cleaned the cut and began to bandage it Scooter asked, "How'd you learn to do that?"

"This I learned while working in a hospital. It's a cinch. You know what's really hard, though?" John smiled and bounced his eyebrows up and down like Groucho Marx. "Big medicine."

"Could you teach me *that?*"

John ruffled Scooter's hair. "When we get some time, you bet."

Scooter wouldn't take no for an answer. "Geez, John, don't be like Mike. He always tells me 'Later.'"

John sighed and dropped his shovel. "Okay, break time."

The two of them sipped water from paper cups and sat on the ground with their backs against a truck tire.

"So," said John, "you want to know how to be a healer?"

Scooter nodded, his mouth full of water.

"First lesson, think of a time when you hurt inside. No bandage in the world could make that feel better, right?"

Scooter shook his head. "Like the time I got in trouble for cheating on my spelling test. My teacher was so mad, and Mom looked like she would cry. I hated feeling that way."

John took the little boy's hands in his, and continued. "Tell me what happened to your hurt."

Scooter blinked several times, then smiled. "I was grounded for a week and had to do a bunch of extra chores for Charlene. The next day I had to take a new test and I got a gold star 'cause I got almost all of them right. I told Mom I wouldn't cheat again and she hugged me and said I should pray and tell Heavenly Father that too."

John released the boy's hands and nodded. "Your peace came back. The hurt was gone."

"Where did it go?"

"When you said you were sorry, and that you'd never cheat again, Jesus took your pain so you wouldn't have to hurt anymore."

Scooter looked up at the sky. "Is that why when I give my mom a hug sometimes, when she's sad, she feels better afterwards?"

John nodded. "And for a moment there, don't you feel sad with her?"

"Yeah."

"And then," John continued, "through the Atonement of Jesus Christ, the sadness is taken away and replaced with warm, happy feelings."

"Yeah," said Scooter. "Does that always work?"

"Not as much or as soon as we would like sometimes. God has his own timetable for things. Sometimes we have to hurt. It helps us grow in special ways—makes us strong."

"Yeah, I suppose."

"Just remember, Scooter, He's always there when you need Him. Even when you feel all alone, and things hurt so much you can't see how it could ever feel better, the Savior is always there for you."

Two male voices interrupted John and Scooter.

"What is the point of laying down a mountain of these sandbags if the water is just going to go higher?"

"So what are you planning to do, just leave?"

Scooter and John turned to see the two gray-haired, middle-aged men arguing. They were neighbors in the town, and part of the hand-over-hand line that passed filled sandbags up to the flood wall.

"It beats fighting the river and losing. Nobody should have built on this ground anyway. It's too low. It really belongs to the river."

"That's easy for you to say, you're from California. Out there you got earthquakes. And when things get knocked down, you just build over the remains. But we don't live like that here."

"Yeah, I know. Everybody here thinks once they lay down some roots, that's it. The land is theirs forever. Well it isn't. The land doesn't really belong to anyone."

"Oh, please! Spare me your new age, 'the earth is my mother,' garbage. Dirt is dirt, and the river is the river, and people have to live where they can."

"There's just no getting through to you, is there? Fine, you stay here and keep sandbagging until the water reaches your nose. But don't come running to me when it's all over."

"Fat chance of that. I'd rather drown first."

"That is a definite possibility!"

Scooter frowned. John shook his head, then smiled as the two men continued right on working together as a team. Obviously their discussion had just been the newest chapter in a long-running disagreement and was probably meant as a distraction.

When they went back to work, Scooter asked, "Is this going to work? Will the flood wall hold?" He was holding the next sandbag, while John dumped shovelfuls of sand into it.

"Hope so. We better pray it does, because there's a whole lot of water coming down this way."

Scooter laid the half-filled bag down and ran over to stand on top of the new bags that formed a thin rim on the creek flood wall. His young eyes scoured the river valley northward, but the flood was still too far away to be seen. His face crinkled up.

"How long until it gets here?" he asked, coming back to John.

"Should be showing up by tomorrow sometime."

In all of Scooter's eight and a half years, there had never been a time when life went smoothly. There was always something to worry about, especially in his mother's life. Surrounded now by so many worried people, Scooter's empathic alarms were sounding constantly. He was wound as tight as a spring, and near to breaking.

John stopped shoveling and put his arm around the boy.

"We know the flood is coming, don't we?"

Scooter nodded.

"Well, you know if we stay calm, do our very best, and prepare ourselves to face our fears, we'll be okay. That's when the Lord can step in to help us. It's when we run away from what frightens us that things get worse, because we don't ever get stronger or braver then. Does that make sense to you?"

Scooter nodded again. "I think so. I was afraid of this boy, Doyle, back in Chicago. And Mike told me I had to stand up to him or Doyle would never leave me alone."

"Did it work?"

"Yup. I got a black eye, but Doyle liked me after that. My mom was mad at Mike though, 'cause he told me I had to be willing to fight Doyle."

John began shoveling as he talked. "Most trouble comes from trying to run away from a problem, not in facing it. We might get a black eye if we face our troubles, but then it's done and over with and we can go on. If we run away, we're just giving the trouble a chance to grow bigger and eventually it'll catch up with us. Only then it might give us more than just a black eye!" John grinned at Scooter and reached out to tousle his hair. "Got that?"

Scooter grinned back at John. "I guess so. But it don't matter. I like you anyway, John. You're a good guy!"

John laughed.

* * *

Dave Mosely finally convinced the Army Corps of Engineers that cutting a hole in the river levee just north of Hampton Corner was the only chance of saving the town. A barge crane was floated upriver even before the official permission was granted. The following day, Tuesday, August 3, 1993, water from the river would be allowed into the Tillman River Valley for the sole purpose of diverting the flood now making its way down the valley from Valmeyer.

People like the MacFarlands raced against the clock to save as much as they could before the water got to their homes. News reporters were all over the place, documenting the struggles for the rest of the country and the world. Some of them even pitched in on the sandbagging. Government officials in Washington passed emergency legislation to provide disaster relief for the victims of America's worst flooding disaster.

# chapter 10

The levee crew worked straight through the night. Under the glow of halogen lights, they feverishly fought to construct a defense against the coming flood. Predictions said the flood would reach Hampton Creek by Wednesday night. And by Tuesday morning a new element was added to the drama.

Three and a half miles upriver from the town, a huge crane swung out from a flat-bottomed barge and dropped a scoop the size of a station wagon onto the levee north of the town. The crane's scoop bit into the intact part of the levee. They were planning to make a 400-foot breach, a hole in the levee longer than a football field. It would take some time and would be worth it if it worked. But would it?

Even as the scoop took out enough of the levee that the first bit of Mississippi River flowed into the river valley and began moving downhill toward the Hampton Creek flood wall, more of the valley northward was being swallowed up.

On a road that came down from the hills, a woman standing near a roadblock checkpoint yelled at one of Raymond Floyde's deputies. Pointing down into the valley, she said, "Why didn't someone tell us? We still have stuff down there we need to get out." Even as she spoke, not a half mile away in the lower valley, she saw her farmhouse shudder, slowly turn off of its foundation, then float off. In a moment it rolled over onto one side and collapsed.

"Oh!" she cried out, hands to her mouth. "Oh, no!"

All the color drained of out her face, and she slumped up against the deputy. "It's gone. It's all gone."

\* \* \*

On Monday Mike Torres did what he could on the creek flood wall. On Tuesday he stayed put at the motel. As if thinking about the damp places behind the motel could dry them out, he fretted and worried for hours.

Linda also did what she could at the creek flood wall until way after dark. Strangely, she found Mike already up and gone when she awoke Tuesday morning. She hardly had time to think about Mike's absence when a sharp pain in her abdomen replaced the usual morning sickness. Knowing that fresh air would help a little, she stood on the toilet to hang her head out the window there.

Just as she pulled her head in, something caught her eye. Right behind the café she saw Mike poking at something on the ground with his crutch. The crutch sank into the ground until it was half covered. When Mike pulled it out, he angrily flung it away from him, where it bounced off the levee that formed a loose C behind the motel.

Linda dressed and hurried out to talk to her husband.

\* \* \*

John had not slept. After tucking a worn-out Scooter into bed at the motel, he went back to work on the creek flood wall. There, his calm, steadfast tone helped sooth the nerves of those around him. Sometimes he cracked jokes; a couple of times he led people in a cheerful song.

He had done nothing spectacular. He simply acted as if he knew God was helping the effort—which he did. Talking about God was much easier when people were facing a crisis. Their hearts were more open, their pride weakened. John felt sad that it sometimes took a disaster to get people thinking about God, but then again, if a disaster *did* bring people closer to God, wasn't that a blessing? He knew it was.

That morning Charlene had cooked him a quick breakfast of hash browns and eggs. His hunger amply satisfied, John came out the back door of the café and noticed Linda arguing with Mike around the back of the main building. One of Mike's crutches had mud on it.

He stretched with arms held wide, and then ambled over to where he could hear the argument.

"Why didn't you tell me? Don't you trust me even now?" Linda was mad. Really mad. Quiet, calm, gentle Linda was showing a side John hadn't seen before. "I deserve to know."

"I didn't want you worrying."

"So when were you going to tell me? When everything slid into the river?"

"That's not going to happen. We might get some more water up here. It could even cause a problem on the back rooms, but—"

"*When* were you going to tell me?"

Mike looked down at the ground. "When were you going to tell me you're pregnant?"

Linda blinked, stopped short in her anger. "How did you know?"

"Well, let me see. There's throwing up in the morning, and you've been acting different . . . and you just *seem* different. I didn't know for sure. I didn't really know until just now."

Linda touched his arm. "Are you mad at me?"

Mike changed instantly. "What? No! Why would you think that?"

Linda slid her arms around him and put her face up against his chest. "We didn't really talk about it. I thought maybe you would be upset, or worried, or . . . I don't know."

Softly he kissed her ear. "It is a wonderful gift. What more could I want?"

John appeared then from around the corner of the building and walked over to the large mud area. He knelt down and poked at the soupy mess. "Looks like the river wants to come visit you. Maybe we should tell somebody about this." Rising, he met Mike's eyes. "Don't you think?"

Linda quickly became serious. "He's right, Mike. We're going to need help here."

Mike shook his head. "Nobody is going to help us. It's not worth it to them."

"Of course they'll help." Linda pointed toward the creek flood wall. "The whole town has been working together. All we have to do is . . ."

"No. They'll all say this piece of land is too unstable. And they'd be right. Linda, no one should have built on it. We'll be lucky if the whole place doesn't fall down on us before this is through."

Linda couldn't believe her ears. She glanced at John.

"It looks like he's right. But you never know until it's over."

"There has to be something we can do. My aunt's gift . . ."

Mike stopped her. "Your aunt knew, I'm sure she did. But how often does a flood like this happen? Once in a hundred years, five hundred? The odds, that's what people play."

The three of them looked at each other, wondering.

Finally John said, "I'll go tell the man from the engineer corps. He'll want to know. In the meantime, Linda, maybe you ought to prepare just in case you have to leave."

Linda flushed angrily. "We're not leaving, and that's that!" She looked from one man to the other, feeling overwhelmed and unsure of herself. "This is our home . . ." her voice trailed off. She didn't know what to say.

John looked deep into Mike's eyes for a moment, nodded, and left to find Dave.

* * *

In a while John came back with Dave Mosely, Raymond Floyde, and Mayor Smooty. After looking at the mud behind the motel, Dave shook his head sadly at Mike and Linda. "I wish I had something encouraging to tell you. The water pressure on the flood wall has liquified the base of the wall, and it's soaking through to this side. Whoever filled in this spot didn't put in enough of a rock substrate. What I mean is, the water is coming up from the bottom, so the soil molecules are losing touch with each other. That's what happens to dirt when it turns into quicksand. The dirt particles can't grab hold of each other, so everything becomes unstable."

At the mention of "quicksand," Mayor Smooty instinctively stepped back a couple of steps. When no one else moved, he blushed and came back to the group.

"Can't we pile some fill or gravel on it?" asked Raymond.

"Won't do any good." Dave picked up a handful of the mud and rolled it around in his fingers. "At this point, the water will just soak through anything we pile on here. And sandbags won't help the building foundations. This piece of ground was originally lower than the river, or at least close to the same level. The river has filled in between the levees over the years. This place between the river and creek was probably once all marshy."

Smooty, who had lived in Hampton Corner all his life, agreed. "It was. I remember as a kid hunting leopard frogs right where we stand. But that was before you Army Corps guys set out to 'tame' the Mississippi. Back in the '30s most of the levees and locks were created around these parts. Things have changed a lot around here since then."

"Should we evacuate the motel?" asked Raymond.

"I would," said Dave. "Ground's too unstable to trust right now. The building might come through okay, and then again, it could go all at once."

Mike had not said a word while the group was looking over the problem. And then, as Linda looked for her husband to find some other way to save their dreams, he just turned and walked away. She felt abandoned.

Linda looked from one face to another, scared. John put a comforting arm around her and said, "Go be with Mike. You've got some plans to make."

\* \* \*

That night John patrolled the creek flood wall carrying a propane lantern with him, checking for leaks. In twenty minutes, at midnight, his watch would be over. The night was quiet, with most of the town evacuated; only the sandbagging crews still worked, and they moved quietly too. Frogs and crickets sang loudly.

Dave appeared out of nowhere, looking up at the full moon. "Pretty night."

"Shouldn't you be sleeping?" asked John.

"Yeah. Tried to, but I guess I've been fighting it too long."

The two men walked along the flood wall together.

"Pass the word," said Dave. "Don't worry about a slow trickle of clear water. But if the water's cloudy, that means material is getting washed out of the levee underneath you. Now that we've got water coming in from two holes, things will change fast."

John saluted. "Gotcha, general. Can do."

Dave smiled weakly. "It does feel like the military. I can't wait to get back to . . ." His words trailed off into the dark. "I don't know, maybe I'm getting too old for this kind of thing."

John could sense the weariness in the man. He put his hand up on Dave's shoulder. "Maybe you're too tired. Why don't you try to get some sleep." Dave nodded, and in moments the engineer could barely keep his eyes open. He straggled off toward a trailer that belonged to the corps, barely making it into bed. It was the first time since the disaster had begun that he slept soundly.

Soon John handed off the lantern to his relief man, repeated the instructions, and moved off toward the town park. Kneeling down on a patch of especially plush grass, he prayed at length. He expressed all of his concerns and desires. As the Savior had promised John, saying, "The Comforter, which is the Holy Ghost, . . . will bring all things to your remembrance,"[4] inspiration and comfort came in the form of a memory.

*The other apostles remained, reclined about the table of the Last Supper, their heads resting on each other's shoulders. Judas had left abruptly at the Lord's words, and though the eleven looked soberly from one to another, confusion and doubt in the exchange of each glance, they sensed it was not the time for questions. There was an urgency about the Master's next words, and he left no room for other matters. He was leaving them. The thought struck panic in John's heart—what would they do without Him, where would they go, why was He leaving? The Lord could stop the elements with a word, surely He feared nothing . . .*

*But in his heart, John knew it was he that feared and not the Lord. And then the Savior answered that very fear: "Peace I leave with you, my peace I give unto you: not as the world giveth, give I unto you. Let not your heart be troubled, neither let it be afraid . . ."[5] And somehow, John was not afraid, knowing the Lord would still be with him, guiding him.*

Touched by the memory, John cried openly. In that moment, all was right, all was peaceful and calm. All was as it needed to be.

The tears ran down John's cheeks, and the words filled his heart. Through the sorrow came yet another testimony of God's glory. Hope rose through the deep waters of affliction. There was healing and peace.

And at last, when the tears had stopped, he simply lay down on the open lawn and quickly fell asleep.

# c h a p t e r   1 1

Early Wednesday morning birds sang loudly in the trees. The sun came out once again, shining benignly upon the water-filled land. John was sitting in the front of a small boat, while Raymond Floyde sat in the back, running the outboard motor. The two of them were surveying the flooded river valley between Valmeyer and Hampton Corner.

Authorities had sealed off access to the valley after the river levee was breached the day before. A 400-foot hole now allowed the Mississippi to pour into the valley less than four miles from Hampton Corner. Now the two arms of the flood had become one. The Tillman River Valley was all underwater, and pressure was building on the Hampton Creek flood wall. Several leaks had begun worrying those that remained in the small town. Despite workers' efforts to pump the water back into the flooded valley, a pool was growing in the northwest corner where the Starbright Motel sat.

Raymond and John were looking for farmers who had slipped past the roadblocks to get back to their homesteads. They planned to help those who refused to leave, or turn back those who just needed a little coaxing. For some reason Raymond felt better with John along.

"You sure they don't need you more back in town?" asked Raymond over the noise of the small boat motor.

"They'll be okay." John kept his eyes peeled through the binoculars Raymond had given him. "Looks like there are some pigs over there on that roof."

Raymond turned in the direction John pointed. It was in the predawn darkness that John had showed up at Raymond's home, knocking on the door before Raymond was even dressed. John's offer to help out in the valley had surprised the undersheriff, since he'd only told Sheriff Picou the night before about his plan to go out in the morning.

Raymond's thoughts drifted to his family. They were staying at their bishop's home in Waterloo while there was danger the creek flood wall wouldn't hold. He had talked to his wife last night. One of the girls was having nightmares. Raymond felt helpless; he couldn't even help his own family, let alone the whole town.

"That's the MacFarland place. A bunch of his land is down in a low hollow," said Raymond, pointing at some buildings behind a row of oak trees. "I would have thought for sure he would have gotten all his animals out."

John nodded. "Guess they ran out of time, just like the rest of us."

There were around thirty pigs on top of a shed roof, crowded together on one end. As John and Raymond reached the shed, John scrambled up onto the roof and worked on coaxing a pig into the boat. As Raymond worked to keep the boat steady for John, another, larger boat came around the half-drowned oak trees behind the shed and into view. Jeff and Sandy MacFarland were in it.

When the other boat came up to the shed roof, Raymond shook his head. "Guess it won't do any good to say you're not supposed to be here, would it?"

"Nope," answered Jeff, as he hopped out of the boat and onto the roof. "Got work to do here. You can get on my case later. No way am I gonna let you do my job for me!"

It was hard, sweaty, exhausting labor. The pigs were terrified of the flood waters, but they were just as afraid of the boats. More than once, one of them would wriggle free, jump out of the boat, and run back up the roof.

"For two cents I'd shoot these ornery things and be done with it," exclaimed Raymond.

One particularly difficult sow shoved Jeff off the roof and into the water. He came up sputtering and swearing, spitting river water out of his mouth. "Give me a quarter and I'll help you shoot them."

"Fat chance, buster." Sandy pointed her finger at both of them. "Either one of you even tries to hurt my pigs, you'll have to go through me first! I helped *born* those little squealers!"

Jeff, dripping wet, gave a hoot of derision. "*Little?* You better take another look, woman! Maybe you need glasses!" Sandy stuck out her tongue and then retorted, "I may be blind, but I'm not dumb! You don't see *me* wrasslin' the critters!"

"She's got you there, buddy," Raymond said nonchalantly. She gave them one last meaningful glare and turned back to arrange things in the boat. The two men grinned at each other, glad for a bit of humor.

Meanwhile John knew the whole loading process was taking too long. He carefully made his way across the top of the unstable roof to the far end of the hog group, knelt down beside the largest sow, and whispered something. In a moment, he rose and walked back toward the boats. The hog followed him.

Jeff stopped to watch, fascinated.

When John and the pig reached the boat, the pig questioningly smelled all around and on it. John picked up the pig's front legs and set them in the boat. Then, he picked up the hind end and boosted the pig into the boat. The hog didn't make a sound or resist at all.

"How'd you do that?" asked Jeff.

"Pig talk," shrugged John. "The old Soooooeeeeeyyy language. Taught to me by a fine old pig."

"Yeah, sure."

Raymond, wrestling his own protesting load of bacon, wished *he* knew John's secret pig language.

Even in Jeff's bigger boat, no more than five pigs could be taken off the roof at a time. Raymond's smaller craft could only take three. Using a cell phone, Sandy made sure transportation for the pigs would be ready when they got to dry ground, where the twins and Natalie were waiting with a trailer.

Raymond finally asked, "How come your pigs weren't already out of here? Would have thought you wouldn't get stuck like this. You're generally right on top of things, Jeff."

Jeff's jaw tightened. "Kids. Left them to take care of something and they didn't. They spaced it out, and I didn't know until this morning. What's a few thousand dollars in livestock to them?"

Nobody spoke on the way back to get the rest of the pigs.

The two boats came around the oak trees and found a large inboard motorboat at the shed. An old man and a younger woman were trying to get one of Jeff's pigs into their boat.

At first Raymond thought they must be trying to steal the pig. Jeff's face was twisted with anger, his right hand curled into a tight fist beside him, and Raymond worried about real trouble breaking out.

"That's Silas on the roof," said Sandy. "What's he doing here?"

Jeff didn't hear her. All he could see was Kathy. His first love, Kathy. His first wife, Kathy. Mother of his boys, the Kathy who had run off and left all of them.

Sandy immediately sensed the change in Jeff. At first she thought it must be Silas. And then it hit her: the woman with Silas had to be Kathy. Sandy felt as if she had suddenly walked into a deep freeze.

She had been meaning to go see Kathy to better understand her and evaluate what her return to Hampton might mean to Jeff. But what with the levee breaking up at Valmeyer, it just hadn't happened. Now Jeff's past was staring directly into her eyes.

"What are *you* doing here?" Jeff's harsh tone startled everyone.

The pig Silas and Kathy were struggling with escaped and ran back to the others on the roof. Kathy wiped a strand of sweaty hair away from her face. "Still can't let anyone help, can you?" she said.

Jeff saw how thin and frail Kathy had become. The AIDS virus had drained whatever color she still had. There was hardly any resemblance to the pretty, young, foolish woman he had been angry at for so many years. The woman of his memories. The woman he had loved so much that when she left he almost couldn't go on.

Raymond docked his boat, and John jumped out and pulled it up onto the roof. Sandy maneuvered theirs next to the others. When Jeff just stood there, glaring at Kathy, Sandy frowned at him, brushed past, and got out herself to pull the boat up further and secure it safely with a rope.

"I'm Sandy," she said to Kathy, offering a hand to shake. "I don't care what he thinks right now. I'm glad for your help." In reality she wasn't quite sure of how she felt about having this woman here. She was, after all, the one who'd first captured Jeff's heart. But Sandy knew that for everyone's sake she needed to reach out to Kathy.

Kathy smiled weakly and shook the hand offered to her.

"You know," said Sandy, "with all these guys here, maybe you and I, if you're interested, could go over to the house and get some things. I've been worried all night about it."

Kathy looked back at Jeff, who was still in the boat. "Sure. That would be okay."

Jeff looked as if he were going to protest, but then tightened his jaw and turned away from the two women. Sandy tightened her own jaw and waved Kathy toward the boat.

After the women left in the inboard boat, Jeff climbed onto the roof and went up to Silas. "What *are* you doing here? And why in the world did you bring *her?*"

"Your cell phone bled over onto my boat radio while we were helping some other people. Kathy wanted to come. So as soon as we dropped off those other folks, we headed over here. Jeff, she just wants to help."

Jeff bit back the bitter remarks that flooded his heart. "I thought you said she had AIDS?"

"She does, but her doctor says she's in an upturn. She's feeling better." Silas seemed to shrink. "But it won't last."

Jeff noticed Silas was looking older and very worn out. It was as if Kathy's disease was also killing Silas. Despite his intention to stay hard and angry, Jeff couldn't help but feel some pity for the man.

John came by with another pig following him. Silas and Jeff stopped talking until the parade passed. Silas was stunned, too surprised by what he had just seen to comment.

"This isn't right. It's just not right," complained Jeff, refusing to be unnerved by John's trick "She doesn't belong here. She already gave up her chance. Her coming can't change anything now. The time for that was long ago. It's gone, finished."

Silas looked as if Jeff had slapped him. Then he began to cry.

"She wants to make amends for her life," whispered Silas. "It's all she has left now. She just wants to do what she can, while she can. Please don't take that away from her."

Jeff started to protest.

"Jeff, wait. Hear me out. Please." Silas was pleading, his hands shaking from emotion, his voice quavery. "You have a fine wife and children. After this flood, you'll come back from the trouble; you're the type that always bounces back. But Kathy, she has almost nothing now. And I know she brought it on herself . . . she knows it too. She just wants to show how sorry she is for what she's done. Can't you just let her have that much?"

* * *

Sandy tore off the screen on the second floor window and climbed inside. Kathy handed her a rope to tie off the boat to something in the room. Then the two of them waded through thigh-deep water, high-stepping over the carpets, which had floated free. The fourteen feet of water in the hollow where the farm lay was destroying the home.

"This was my son's room. His name was Robbie." Sandy looked around, remembering what the room looked like when her son still lived.

"My father told me about his death. I'm sorry," Kathy said. She remembered the house well. It had been so long since she had allowed herself to think about it.

"This was the twins room when I . . ." said Sandy.

Sandy and Kathy looked at each other; they knew they were bound together by a man, two boys, and almost impossible hopes. Kathy nodded. "I remember."

Embarrassed by her mistake, Sandy blushed a vivid red. "Of course you do. How stupid of me." An uncomfortable silence filled the flooded room.

Sandy broke it first. "I'm looking for a box. One with red writing on it, saying something like, family photos, or . . . I thought I loaded it up yesterday, but I couldn't find it later. It's got most of our family albums, yearbooks, and Robbie's football trophies in it. If anything happens to it, I don't know what I'll do."

Sandy choked up. All of the stress of the past few days finally swelled up inside of her. She started crying. "I'm sorry. I don't know what's come over me. I'll be fine."

Kathy hesitated a moment, watching the woman's shoulders shake from the sobs she was trying to repress, then put her arms around Sandy. "I'm glad . . ." Kathy started in a weak voice. "I'm glad my boys had you to look after them." They both wept. Sandy for the memories she was afraid of losing, and Kathy for the memories she'd never built. In their shared pain, the two women began to feel an ease of heart. At last a little of the long ache from all of their pasts was being laid to rest. Finally, perhaps, there could be some healing. For all of them. God was opening the door, now all they had to do was step through it.

\* \* \*

On the next trip out with more pigs, John went with Jeff. John had maneuvered it that way so he could talk to Jeff. Besides, putting Silas and Jeff together would have made them both uncomfortable.

John dipped his hand down into the churned up flood waters for a moment. He had spent most of his early life living beside water. The Sea of Galilee was almost his earliest memory. A small body of water, only eight miles wide at the northern end, and fourteen miles long, it was shallow—only one hundred and fifty-seven feet deep. After winter storms the sea had been the same color as these flood waters.

John had been an offhand fisherman, helping his older brother James in the family business. He hadn't ever come to love fishing, but he could never get very far away from water. Even now, so many years later, he could remember the king fishers and blue herons that always followed the boats, looking for a handout. And when the fishermen brought their catch back up on the beach, the small crustaceans, locally known as "beach fleas," would make pests of themselves. The smell of tilapia would be part of him forever.

But it was the water more than anything that stayed with him. No matter where he roamed all through the years, it was water that drew him back to himself.

"Must be hard to see your farm like this," said John, loud enough to be heard over the boat motor. "Your family has worked this land for a long time, haven't they?"

Jeff nodded, not really interested in making conversation. Since Sandy and Kathy had gone off together, Jeff had pulled into his deepest shell.

"Ever get time to fish?" John didn't wait for an answer. The gray-and-white pigs were getting restless, so he laid a gentle hand on them. With a few snorts they lay down again in the bottom of the boat.

"My family liked to fish," continued John. "It was their life. We did it as a business. My father and brother, they liked it better than anything else. You know, I tried to. Did my best to like it." John paused, remembering. "Guess I was a bit of a disappointment to them."

Jeff barely listened.

"Then one day someone offered me a different line of work. I tell you, no one had to ask me twice. Quick as a wink, I was out of there. So that just left my brother in the business. I felt a little bad about it, since my father was getting older. Even then he was looking to semi-retire and have his sons take over."

Jeff recognized the parallels to his life. He had not wanted to take over his father's business either. Lighting out for Chicago to learn electronics had been his ticket to freedom. And his older brother had been left to take care of the family business.

"Though, you know, I was never meant to be a fisherman. Those who are, I salute them. You can help others, serve God, and make the world a better place in a lot of different ways. But, pretending to be something you're not . . . that I can't agree with. No, I wouldn't do that to any child of mine." Jeff didn't answer, but mulled over John's words.

After landing, John and Jeff loaded the pigs into the trailers in half the time it took Silas and Raymond and were soon on their way back for more.

"So the woman with the red hair, she was your first wife?"

Jeff looked at John, surprised.

"I heard Raymond and Silas talking."

"Yeah." After a long pause, Jeff went on, "She ran out on me."

"Then she must have come back here to try to make things right. She's dying; you can tell by looking at her. I've seen the look before, many times."

Jeff fidgeted with the motor handle, avoiding John's eyes. "She has AIDS. And I can't say I'm surprised. The life she lived . . . I'd say she earned it."

John looked intently at Jeff. "You don't want to forgive her, do you? A woman like that, running off and leaving her husband, her babies." John shook his head at the thought. "Maybe she doesn't deserve it."

Jeff glared at John. "I don't see as how this is any of your business."

John cocked his head to one side. "Maybe. But I'd say pain doesn't go away just because you change the subject, or tell people they can't talk about it around you."

Jeff frowned deeply. "Look. It's none of your business," he repeated.

"Is it God's business?"

Jeff laughed bitterly. "God! I'm not going to talk to you about God."

"Why? We believe in the same God, Jeff. I understand where you're coming from—and why you struggle so much with it. Your faith that is, and with forgiveness and accepting Christ's mercy."

Frustrated, Jeff yelled, his voice sharp and full of pain. "Who *are* you? Do you get a kick out of messing with other people's lives? Or their heads? Just *shut up* and . . ."

Jeff could have punched John right then if they had been closer. Instead he slammed his foot against the middle gunwale of the boat.

"And what?" John asked quietly, smiling compassionately. "Leave you alone? Your family's been doing that for a long time, Jeff. I'm not blind. You won't even let Sandy talk to you about any of it, and I'd say it's as much her business as yours. But has your way worked? Is your life better? Does Kathy's leaving you and the twins hurt less because you've tried to bury it down deep all these years? Do you feel less guilty over Robbie's death because you refuse to think about him?"

Jeff savagely flipped off the boat motor. They began to coast, then gradually stopped beside a half-drowned tree. "I don't know where you think you can get off talking to me about any of this. And if Sandy told you, she had no business doing it. You don't know nothing about it, and I'm sure as heck not gonna let you dabble in what you know nothing about!"

"I was with Robbie when he died," said John. "I heard his last words, before his spirit went home to God."

Jeff looked at John incredulously. "What? You couldn't have been. There was *nobody* with Robbie. He died alone." The words caught in Jeff's throat. "He . . . on the side of the road where he was thrown when the tire blew."

"I *was* there, Jeff. I was with Robbie when his time ran out. He didn't expect it, none of you did. Everyone's time is running out, Jeff. Just like this flood, life isn't going to wait for you to get ready before it happens. Your boys are growing older, and they're growing away from you because you've stopped living. You've frozen your heart, and you're standing still emotionally. And you're missing the best part of life with them, and with Sandy and Natalie. Jeff, you have to let go of the past and start living in the present so you can hold onto your family before you lose them for good."

Jeff knew it was the truth. The painful burning in his heart confirmed it. But it was painful to hear a perfect stranger say such personal things about his life. It was all he could do to keep from bursting into tears.

Raymond and Silas were coming up quickly behind him in their boat. "Got problems?" called Raymond. "Need a hand?"

Jeff wiped his eyes and waved them off. He restarted the boat motor and shot John an angry look that said, "I'll talk to you later."

John gave him a quiet, calm look that replied, "I'll be around."

* * *

Kathy sat awkwardly near the twins. No one knew what to say. The usually hyperactive, talkative boys now squirmed uncomfortably in their seats. Finally Sandy, knowing that conversation would help take their minds from the loss they would soon know, and from the pain in their pasts, went to rescue them with some easy conversation, asking Kathy what the twins were like as babies. The boys opened up a little as she told a funny story about them learning to crawl, and then pulling on a table cloth trying to stand before they even got crawling down. Jeff cringed when everyone laughed at the inevitable ending of the table cloth slipping and the boys landing flat on their bottoms next to an overturned potted plant. Jeff used the pigs as an excuse to get away. He couldn't stand everyone being so chummy with Kathy. *What about the story that happened two months later?* He thought. *Why don't you tell them that one, Kathy? How I'd have to stay up all night listening to my boys cry and say the only word they had learned yet, "Mama." Why don't you tell them that one?* The bitterness stung his conscience, but he refused to listen to that little voice of reason point out that he had already told that story plenty of times, whether in those words, or in his grumbling and moping actions. He didn't want to hear what he deep down already knew: that there wasn't time for those kinds of stories, and the boys deserved to hear something *good* about the first year of their life, and the woman who gave them that life.

He couldn't tell Sandy how much it hurt to see Kathy, and he sure wasn't about to join the family reunion. So Jeff did what he had always done when life was hard. He bottled up and pulled inside. He wasn't surprised to find himself sitting on top of a rock, looking over the flooded river valley with the bottle of vodka in his hand.

A conversation in his head raged back and forth.

*Why didn't you put your foot down and just tell Sandy? Tell her to stay away from Kathy?*

*Yeah, and like that would have worked.*

*Well, you could have at least told Kathy off, right then and there.*

*Sure, that would have looked classy. Trash the dying woman in front of everyone. Then who's the jerk? She comes across the poor little innocent victim again, like she always has.*

Jeff unscrewed the bottle and almost brought it to his lips. He could smell the liquor, remember the numbing feeling that came with it. And that's all he wanted right then—to get numb and away from everything.

Yet he hesitated and looked up into the sky, wishing an angel would appear to tell him not to drink, not to run away. Because he wanted to believe there was a God. A God who cared, and could help Jeff make something better out his life.

But of course, an angel didn't appear. So Jeff tipped the bottle up, but stopped again before drinking. And then he saw the small white spot floating by in the water.

It just looked like trash that sometimes floated in the flood waters. Jeff squinted, trying to be sure he had seen it move. He shielded his eyes from the sun with his free hand.

It was a long way off, probably more than a hundred yards out into the brown water. And it was moving against the current, in jerks and lurches. That meant it was alive, whatever it was.

Jeff sat the bottle down on the rock and stood. Was that a person out there?

The white spot stopped jerking, and went with the current again. Jeff began walking along the waters edge, keeping pace. Thinking.

He had walked maybe sixty yards, and came around a small hill. Some onlookers, "catastrophe sightseers," were there with binoculars, surveying the flood. One of them pointed and said, "That's a baby cow, a calf out there."

"So much for that side of beef," said another.

Jeff frowned at them.

"Hey, why don't one of you guys go in and get it?" asked a woman. "You're always bragging about what great swimmers you are."

"For a cow? In those flood waters? No way."

"But it's going to drown."

"Better it than me. And besides, it got itself into that mess. It can get itself out."

The last words hit Jeff like a hammer. So many times he had said almost the same thing about Kathy, the twins, anyone who did anything he thought stupid. *They got themselves into the mess. They can get themselves out.*

But the calf. It would surely drown. What difference would it make?

No one else was going to help. And Jeff was a good swimmer. His jaw tightened, and he looked down at the ground, kicked a stone, and then slowly pulled off his work boots and socks.

*I must be an idiot*, he thought, just before heading into the water.

# c h a p t e r    1 2

Those in charge discovered too late that the hole punched into the river levee was too small to do what was intended. Water from the Mississippi flowed in, met the other arm of the flood waters coming down from Valmeyer, then turned even more fiercely toward the Hampton Creek flood wall. Trust and hope in the small wall of sandbags that protected the town diminished, while fear grew.

By noon on Wednesday, 4 August, leakage along the creek flood wall was accelerating despite the huge pumps that had been flown in and set like lifeguards behind the sandbag wall. The lower end of Hampton Corner was partially flooded. And still the flood waters rose.

* * *

"What did they say?" asked Mayor Smooty. He was leaning tiredly with both elbows propped against his pickup truck. It was a ragtag, dirty, and exhausted group that met for a hurried and informal council.

Dave Mosely shook his head. "They said the Corps of Engineers builds levees, they don't blow them up."

"Then we'll do it ourselves," said Herman Mombow.

"I think we're gonna have to," agreed Dave. "I might get fired after all of this, but I don't care anymore. I'm tired of losing. This is one town the river isn't going to get."

Raymond thought about how much dynamite it might take to blow a bigger hole in the levee. "Does anyone know what kind of charge this will take?"

Herman shrugged. "Who's done anything like this before? All I've blown up is my share of tree stumps. What about you, Dave?"

"Nope. I'm in the same boat as you. Guess we'll have to wing it. But whatever we do, we're gonna have to do it fast. Our time is about gone."

Raymond nodded. "Okay, let's do 'er!"

Behind the men, sandbagging efforts were intensifying. Even though there were only twenty-five residents who hadn't yet evacuated, an army of over two hundred workers fought against the flood along the creek flood wall. As the leadership group planned to blow a bigger hole in the river levee, a National Guard helicopter arrived and hovered nearby. The copilot, his back to the open side door of the chopper, strained to throw out filled sandbags as fast as he could while struggling to maintain his balance. Time was of the essence, and there wasn't a lot of it left.

* * *

Kathy and Sandy worked almost as a single person along the Hampton Creek flood wall, grabbing the sandbags that rained down out of the helicopter. Sandy had decided that sitting around feeling sorry about the losses at the farm wasn't going to help. Rounding up the twins and Natalie, she had gone with Kathy to help save the town. Jeff had declined.

On the way back into town, riding in Silas's boat, everyone had inconspicuously studied each other. Silas played captain in front, while Kathy quietly visited with the twins in the back. Sandy and Natalie gave them some privacy by sitting beside Silas.

Now, two hours later, the reunion had been set aside for the battle.

Another helicopter arrived and slowly lowered an inflatable dam over the worst leak in the creek flood wall. Amidst the noise of the helicopter, Jeff pulled up in his truck and stepped out, watching the inflatable dam being lowered into place. Sandy saw him and stopped her sandbagging efforts to watch him, wondering what was going on inside him now. Lifting his eyes, Jeff saw her, and came over.

His clothes were damp, and he looked to Sandy like he had been swimming. She thought of making a joke, but figured it probably wasn't the time.

"So?" she asked, one eyebrow curving upward.

Jeff cocked his head to one side. "Ever feel stupid because you've been acting stupid, then not quite know how to get out of it?" His pants were dripping down along the side of his boots, making a puddle on the ground.

She nodded. "Not as much as you have, obviously, but sure, some. So?"

Jeff squirmed, wishing she would make it easier for him. "I'm sorry."

"Sorry for what?"

"Geez, Sandy! You *know* what! Do you have to make this so hard?" He shook off some water that dribbled down on his hand.

"Yes. Or it won't stick."

The twins came by, pulling a small cart with shovels and empty sandbags in it. They smiled at him and were obviously having a ball. A memory flashed through Jeff's mind of two beautiful little boys playing with a wagon and covered in mud from head to toe, still smiling for all they were worth. *What a waste,* he thought to himself. All the years he could have just enjoyed them, and now they were almost gone. It very nearly broke his heart, thinking about the lost years. If he could do anything at this late date to change all the wasted years, he would, whatever it took. He smiled back at them and waved.

As he turned back to Sandy, she still held him with her eyes. Her jaw was tight with determination, her arms folded tightly across her chest. "Well, Jeff? You were saying?"

Kathy came out from around a National Guard truck. "Hey, Sandy . . ." Seeing Jeff, she stopped abruptly. "Sorry."

As Kathy turned to leave, Sandy caught her arm. "Whoa there, girl. You need to be here right now. Jeff, whatever you have to say, whoever you need to apologize to, you can start with Kathy. She's the one you started out being angry at. The rest of us came later."

Sandy looked pointedly at Kathy and Jeff, then left to follow the twins.

Kathy stood hesitantly, looking as if she would welcome a chance to run. She looked at Jeff with eyes so tired and an expression so weak, Jeff's stomach twisted into a tight knot. What could he possibly say now?

Each waited for the other to speak.

A guardsman came running up to the truck, hopped in, started it, and pulled away. Kathy had to move toward Jeff to get out of the way.

Jeff finally cleared his throat and pushed out the first words that came to him. "So, you talked with the boys?"

Kathy nodded. "They've turned out good. They'll be good men. Sandy did a good job with them. Better than I ever could have." That said, she stopped, waiting to see what would happen next. She fully expected Jeff to agree with her about her poor mothering abilities. But Jeff stood still, his face suddenly full of pain, tears gathering in his eyes. Surprised and shocked, Kathy had an impulse to pull him into her arms and comfort him. It was an impulse she quickly restrained.

"Jeff, I'm sorry. You didn't deserve what happened."

Jeff found he was having trouble breathing. Ragged gasps seemed to be all he could manage. He struggled to take a deep breath, trying to gain control of his jumbled emotions. He wanted to be angry at her and didn't want to. He wanted her to suffer for what she had done, thought she *needed* to suffer for what she had done, and was simultaneously ashamed he was playing judge and jury. Playing God.

Trying to break out of the anger and hurt, he struggled to focus on just the moment. *Pull yourself together, man! This is the here and now, not yesterday!* He cleared his throat and raised his eyes to Kathy. "Your father says . . ." he stumbled and tried again. "You've been sick . . ."

Kathy broke in to rescue him. "Jeff, I have AIDS. I'm going to die, and they say it won't be too long now. That's why I finally came back. I had to, before it was too late. I wanted a chance to ask your forgiveness. Though if you don't forgive me, I can sure understand why. If the tables were turned, I doubt I'd forgive *you*. What I did was really wrong. When I think about how stupid I was, I can hardly believe it. All I could think about was myself. I have no excuse."

Jeff swore and turned away from her. "Why didn't you come before now?"

"Would you have let me? Could I have talked to you and the boys?"

He had no answer but silence.

"That's what I thought. So I stayed away. Besides, quite honestly Jeff, it wasn't until I realized I was dying that I took a look at reality—

till I knew what a selfish little witch I've been. 'Princess Kathy.' That's what some of the girls in high school used to call me. 'Her royal highness, too good for everybody.' I always told myself they were just jealous, but the truth is, they were right. I always did think I was too special for an ordinary life." She laughed harshly. "Well, look how *special* I am now! Guess I got what I really deserved after all."

The tired, sick feeling she had been fighting off rushed back. She thought for a moment she was going to throw up, or faint, or both, but the rush passed, and she stood straight again. Jeff was so wrapped up in his own hurt he hadn't noticed.

"I looked for you," he said, tears now betraying him. He fought hard to stop them, but they ran involuntarily down his cheeks. "Every time you called me, asking to come home, I went out looking, hoping you'd be there when I arrived. But you never were."

"I know. I'm so sorry. I was so screwed up. I wanted to come home, but I was afraid that if I did, I'd somehow lose myself by being a wife and a mommy. I didn't think that would ever be enough for me. I wanted to be a star. I wanted to be someone everyone acknowledged as special, unique. So I stayed away. I chased after rainbows, hung out with all the wrong people. Looked in all the wrong places to find what never existed. I was stupid and too blind to know it. I did love you, Jeff, I did. I just loved myself and my freedom more. I'm sorry. There isn't anything else I can really say."

He couldn't believe his ears. Turning away, he shouted at her, "You were *always* sorry. That was your answer to everything. Anytime you didn't want to grow up and be responsible, you just blew it off, and later said '*Sorry.*' Kathy, some things you just can't do that with!"

She bit her lip. "I know. I mean, at least I do now."

Jeff looked over where the twins were working with Sandy. "They were just babies. You *abandoned* your *babies*. How could you *do* that?"

Kathy stared after the twins, remembering, regretting; and the pain and clear realization of what she had done, what she had lost, washed over her. She broke down and sobbed. Slowly she crumpled to her knees in the dirt, Jeff standing over her, his back stiff, his fists clenched, his jaw tight. Sandy glanced over, saw what was happening, and thought about coming back to help. But her heart said, *No. Give them time and space to work this through.* She turned back to her work, a prayer in her heart. And she cried for both of them. For all of them.

\* \* \*

Natalie was working with John and Scooter on another part of the creek flood wall.

"So your *whole farm* is gone?" asked Scooter in amazement.

"The buildings are probably still there, and the trees," answered Natalie. "And when the flood is over, we can go back and pull it together again. I *hope.*"

"I sure would like to live on a farm." Scooter made a face like a pig, grunting. "Me and the pigs, we could be buddies. I know how to talk pig. John's been teaching me."

Natalie stopped filling her bag, surprised. She glanced at John, who was chuckling at Scooter, then she broke into laughter. The tensions of the moment eased a little.

As Natalie and Scooter were "talking pig," John was very aware of Kathy and Jeff.

John saw Kathy on the ground, sobbing, and Jeff standing nearby. "If you ever loved her," John whispered to Jeff, "then help her now. Reach out, Jeff, reach out. For both your sakes." He knew the Spirit was whispering the same, and he prayed that Jeff was listening.

\* \* \*

Jeff looked across the way into John's eyes, and heard the words as clearly as if the two men were standing next to each other. Anger and forgiveness fought within him. Only one could possess him. The outcome of the rest of his life would hinge on what he chose to do at that moment. How could he truly love Sandy and his children—the way they needed to be loved—if he couldn't let go of this old hurt, the bitterness and anger he had carried for so long?

His own will had to be left behind. It would do him no good now to carry those stubborn beliefs into the future. His ideas about "justice" had to be put aside.

As he struggled with the opposing feelings within him, he suddenly remembered very clearly a scripture his wife had read him, in chastisement, when he was complaining about Silas a few months earlier. It drifted gently into his mind, and he could hear it, as if someone were speaking it to him: "Wherefore, my beloved brethren, if ye have not charity, ye are nothing. . . . charity is the pure love of Christ, and it endureth forever; and whoso is found possessed of it at the last day, it shall be well with him."[6]

Slowly he reached out to Kathy. Then, he gently pulled her into his arms. Her clothes absorbed water from his still-wet clothes.

Sandy watched, glad. If Jeff was ever going to be all hers, then he had to do this. He had to care about Kathy as a precious human being, a person of worth—so he could let go of her, stop obsessing about her. He had to care enough about her to be able to forgive her. Then, and only then, would he be able to truly let her go, without any lingering anger or resentment.

But she was afraid too, knowing the terrible hold Kathy had held on Jeff all these years. She knew Kathy couldn't have had that effect if Jeff hadn't loved her so deeply. What a double bind this was! Jeff must forgive Kathy to love Sandy with his whole heart, but if Jeff finally let go of the anger and hurt, would he still love Sandy? Or would his love return back to Kathy?

It was too much to think of, too terrifying to bear alone, and Sandy clasped her hand to her mouth, suppressing a choked cry. *Oh, help him, God,* she pled in her heart. *Help me. Help us all.*

Kathy shook inside Jeff's arms, flinging her own arms tightly around him. "I'm sorry. *I'm so sorry.*" Sobs wracked her so deeply she could hardly talk. She held to Jeff as if her life depended on it. "I know it's not enough, I know it. It's so stupid to even say it, but I don't know what *else* to say."

"Shhh . . . shhh." He rocked her back and forth as he had done so long ago when she was frightened. He had been glad to be the strong one then, her rescuer, her white knight. It had made him feel like a man. Now, here he was again, but his feelings were different now. Now he *was* a man, not an immature boy any longer.

"Kathy, listen. It wasn't all you."

Suddenly Jeff saw how the two of them had built a fantasy life together. Each had tried to be what they were not, but Jeff had been better at it than Kathy. Each had just wanted to be loved, fully and completely for who they were, but Jeff had been better at sacrificing dreams for whatever had to be done to make life work. Life had been hard—the responsibilities of finances, home, family—particularly so for the very young and inexperienced newlyweds.

Kathy had run away, but Jeff had already run away inside himself even before Kathy had stepped out the door.

Shocked, Jeff realized he'd actually planned it all out in his mind, all those years ago. At some point, he had determined Kathy was going to be the darling princess for him, and he would be her handsome, fearless knight. But she was also supposed to be something more real. She was supposed to make everything perfect at home and make Jeff happy. And somehow she was to make up for Jeff's own lost dreams, for the life he never got to have away from the farm.

Finally, his own anger put aside, his fantasy world destroyed, Jeff could see it all clearly. Now he could see what *he* had done to Kathy, all the pain he put her through because of his own immaturity, his own selfishness, his own impossible expectations. He had driven her off by having such a tight hold on the door to her gilded cage. He had ignored her needs, dreams, and fears and had tried to force his own needs and dreams upon her. Whatever wrong choices Kathy may have made, had been compounded with his own. It wasn't all her fault, not by a long shot.

Jeff held Kathy tenderly, and explained softly what he now saw so clearly, asking her forgiveness and freely forgiving her. Kathy stayed near him, listening, seeing the truth of what he said, answering softly from time to time, and strength and hope seemed to flow back into her as they stood together in each other's arms.

After a bit, Jeff looked up over Kathy's head, and saw Sandy, watching silently, patiently, alone. She raised an eyebrow, then nodded at him encouragingly. A hesitant smile played about her lips, and Jeff came back to the present, understanding the past, and seeing just a hint of what the future would be.

# chapter 13

As dynamite charges were being inserted into the north end of the hole in the river levee, Linda Torres threw a porcelain figurine against the bathroom door.

"I'm not leaving," yelled Linda.

"Yes, we are," Mike yelled back.

Abruptly Linda grasped her belly and doubled over as a sharp pain shot through her.

Mike let go of his crutches and caught her before she fell to the floor, easing her down on their bed. Losing his own balance, he landed beside her.

"Honey? What's the matter?" He propped himself up on one elbow and touched Linda's face.

Linda panted, using the Lamaze breathing techniques she had learned for Scooter's birth. It helped, but the pain didn't end. "I don't know," she finally gasped. "It feels like something is tearing inside."

Suddenly, nothing mattered to Mike but his fear of losing Linda. "We need to get you to a doctor."

She shook her head. "Mike, I've just finally made up my mind. I won't lose the motel. I won't," she groaned. "I'm tired of running. I don't want to go anywhere, I just want to stay here. Mike, this is our *home.*"

Mike smiled weakly. "That's my line. You're supposed to be the sensible one, remember? Besides, what would we do if we stayed? We can't stop the water by sheer force of will."

Another sharp pain tore through her. Eyes widening, she screamed in pain.

There was no one else in the deserted motel complex—or in that part of town—to hear. Everyone else had already left. The only way out now was by boat, or by wading through filthy, treacherous, chest-deep water. Mike was afraid it might even be too late to get out.

Cold sweat dripping down his face, he tried to think calmly. But Linda's expression frightened him. It looked more like the face of a cornered animal than that of his sweetheart. "Honey?"

She gripped his hand so hard he thought the bones in his hand would break. When her pain passed, she let go of his hand and he rubbed it to get the circulation back. "Mike, I can't go. I *can't.*"

"We've been fighting about this for two days now," said Mike. "And ever since that hole behind us in the levee opened up you've been pulling away from me. The bigger the seepage out back grows, the quieter you've become."

"But—"

"No. It's my turn. Hear me out." Mike sat up so he could think clearly. "Linda, you keep saying you want to *be* someone," he said slowly. "Me too. But honey, I finally figured out that where we live isn't what makes us somebody." He stopped as his voice caught. Then he slowly continued with words Linda never thought she'd hear from him. "I finally felt it the other night, and . . . and I prayed. I just feel like it's who we are in God's eyes that counts. So, we have to trust in God. What's most important is what He wants for us, not what we want for ourselves. That, and being together as a family. We don't need this motel to be a family. We just need God."

Linda's heart ached for her husband and for all he had been through. She finally saw how much he loved her and Scooter, and she loved him all the more for it. "I want to be yours forever," she said, eyeing him carefully for his response. This time he didn't look irritated or change the subject. He just held her close. She was about to add something more when a burning, sharp pain ripped through her again. For several minutes she could only groan in agony as Mike held her.

As the pain subsided, Linda lay exhausted and limp in his arms. He held her gently, thinking, worrying, and finally praying.

Suddenly, there was a loud blast from the emergency siren in town. "Linda, that's the final warning signal. They're going to blow the levee. We've got to get out of here, *now.*"

\* \* \*

The three men backed off fifty yards in their boat from the river levee. The dynamite was connected to a radio detonator they had with them.

"Everybody ready?" asked Raymond Floyde.

"So, who pushes the button?" asked Herman Mombow.

"Why don't we let Dave do it," said Raymond.

Dave Mosely looked back at the levee, considered the negative effect this would likely have on his career with the Army Corps of Engineers, and smiled. "Yeah, let me."

He pushed the button. A split second later, the first charge went off, then the second, the third and fourth in rapid succession. The flow of water out of the Tillman River Valley increased immediately and substantially. Raymond struggled to pull the boat back to safer, calmer water. It was obvious *something* significant was happening. Now, would it be enough to take the pressure off the creek flood wall?

A tremor from the explosions moved down the valley and into the deserted town. On the creek flood wall nearest the Mississippi River, a gaping hole suddenly appeared beneath the oldest part as flood water took hold and pushed backward.

In seconds, a thirty-foot gap opened up, and water pushed up against the almost abandoned Starbright Motel.

\* \* \*

Linda was too weak to resist Mike as he carried her as best he could out of their second-floor motel suite. His leg was still not fully healed, and the pain was intense as he put weight on his leg inside the walking cast, but that didn't matter now. He had heard the explosions and the sound of the water roaring through the levee break right behind them. He had no doubt as to what that meant.

They had only moments to get into the rowboat tied up at the bottom of the stairs. Mike prayed the walls of the motel would hold against the water long enough for them to make it.

He had to slide down the stairs with Linda in his arms. The pain in his leg felt like the heat from a blast furnace, but Linda was too hurt to give him any help. She was too weak and close to losing consciousness. Before they reached the boat Linda uttered the words "I'm sorry . . . I'm so sorry," then fainted.

With a groan, the back end of the building collapsed. Mike fumbled with the rope, frantically trying to pull the boat toward them. When he finally got hold of it, he heard another sound that froze his very soul.

The rest of the creek flood wall, going west to meet up with the river levee, gave way. In seconds, fifty feet of the river levee turned to mud and began its trip south toward the Gulf. The motel complex was now part of the river.

Saturated for weeks, the underlying ground bubbled up as the quicksand Dave Mosely had talked about. With no time left, the powerful flood waters surged around the motel, swallowing everything in its path.

"Oh Lord! Linda!" Mike cried out, pulling the limp body of his wife to him, his arms wrapped desperately around her. He continued to pray as the current carried them away. He knew he had to believe his own words now. He had to trust in God and know that everything would be okay, no matter what happened. "Take care of Scooter," was the last plea he managed before the dark waters overtook them.

* * *

Jeff had driven Kathy to her father's hilltop home overlooking the town and the two of them sat in his truck talking for nearly an hour. Despite finally finding some peace, Kathy's strength had ebbed away until she couldn't sit up anymore. Silas opened his front door to find Jeff carrying Kathy in his arms, and the two men needed no words between them as they put her to bed.

Back at the flood wall, Sandy saw Jeff step out of his pickup. She walked over to the truck, carefully searching Jeff's face. "How is she?"

"Not good. She used up a lot of time today." He raised his eyes to look deeply into hers.

Sandy smiled at him, sensing the change in his heart, and reached out hesitantly to caress his cheek with a muddy hand. "You're a good man, Jeff MacFarland. But then, I always knew that." Without a word, Jeff pulled Sandy into his arms and buried his face in her hair as he pulled her as tightly into his body as was humanly possible.

Natalie came running up to them, followed by Scooter, who was pretending to be a wild pig.

"Mom, save me!" squealed Natalie, hiding behind Sandy.

Right then, the creek flood wall further down behind the motel gave way. The roaring, grinding sounds of tons of earth and rock breaking loose caught every worker's attention. All turned to watch as the motel sagged, collapsed, and was swallowed by the waters.

Scooter's eyes grew wide. "My mom!" he screamed. Terrified, he began to run toward the motel.

John came running up behind him, scooping Scooter into his arms.

"John, put me down! I gotta go help my mom and Mike! Lemme go!" Scooter shrieked as he kicked and struggled to be free, tears flowing freely in his terror.

John pulled Scooter in close to him, speaking so softly into Scooter's ear that no one but Scooter could hear his words. He held Scooter firmly, lovingly, until slowly, his struggles ebbed and John was left with a sobbing boy in his arms. Horrified, Jeff and Sandy watched helplessly, their eyes moving back and forth from the devastated child to the spot where the motel had once stood. Nothing remained above the water.

"Jeff, Sandy, take care of Scooter," said John. Handing Scooter into Jeff's arms, John sprinted off.

* * *

The river broke loose at last from the walls that had held it back. Like a ravaging monster set free, it grabbed for all it could.

John was looking at the place where the motel had been, when Jeff ran up beside him. Further back on safer ground, a crew of sandbaggers looked on.

"The boy thinks his parents were in the motel," said Jeff.

John took so long to answer that Jeff thought he hadn't heard. "They were."

Jeff stared at John. "How can you be sure? Maybe they got out in time."

John turned and looked deeply into Jeff's eyes. "Jeff," he said gently, "they were in there when the water hit the motel."

Jeff stepped back. Somehow, he also knew that John spoke the truth. "Then we better notify the authorities."

"Yeah, you do that."

Jeff was still trying to figure John out. Much of what John had said to him out in the boat was true. Okay, it was all true. And those words of truth had lead him to forgive Kathy and himself. But most people didn't talk that way. And they didn't know the kind of details John knew. So who was he? More to the point, *what* was he?

"This didn't have to happen," said John softly. "They waited too long. Most of us wait too long. We always think we have all the time in the world. But we don't. We have so little time. Less than we ever know." He shook his head sadly, wiping a tear from his eye. "God keeps trying to tell us we don't have much time, but we insist on using what little we do have for such silly, useless purposes. Pride, selfishness, revenge, materialism. What a waste. What a terrible, tragic waste."

John turned and put a hand on Jeff's shoulder. "I'm glad you finally saw the truth about Kathy. She did love you, as best she knew how. The woman you forgave today would never have run away and left you and your boys. But she can't change all that now. Her time here is nearly over. We can't go back, only forward."

Jeff's throat grew tight, and his heart beat rapidly.

"You gave her the best gift today you've ever given her, Jeff. The gift of love. What you did for her will make her leaving much easier. If I were you, I'd let the twins be with her tonight. She has very little time left. And Jeff, don't sorrow too much for that. God gave that special gift to Kathy: the awareness of what little time she had left here, and the opportunity to finally face her life before she left. *That* is a very precious gift. One that many people don't get. And fortunately, it was a gift for you too—to take care of the hurt now, while you still have time left to grow and love and to give to your family as you never have in the past."

John paused and looked closely at Jeff. "Pretty good gift."

After John walked away, Jeff stood alone on what was left of the side of the flood wall, watching the water. Slow tears flowed down his face. *Man, I've been doing an awful lot of crying lately. Never cried so much in my life. Am I getting soft?* He wiped roughly at his face with his sleeve. *No,* a soft voice whispered back at him, *You're finally becoming strong in all the right ways.*

He felt so ashamed of the walls he had built around his heart and mind. Walls against the very people he loved the most. Walls against his own children, his own wife. All done in his determination to never let anyone hurt him again the way Kathy had. Instead, he had used his prideful anger to hurt others.

When he finally turned to go back, Sandy was standing a ways behind him, watching and waiting.

They looked at each other, seeing in each other's eyes what each needed to see.

# chapter 14

It didn't take long before everyone knew the second dynamite blast on the river levee had failed. The flood water rushing down the river valley still had no hole large enough to escape through. By six in the evening on Wednesday, the flood workers were having to hold down each new sandbag with their foot until they could put another one on top as water poured over and around the sandbags.

Raymond Floyde directed a search effort to evacuate what was left of the townspeople to higher ground. One man was found in water almost to his neck, holding tightly to a nearby fence line for support as he struggled to make his way to higher ground, his yellow cat perched on his shoulders. "Couldn't leave my best friend," he said.

One family had tried to make their own levee around their house out of plastic sheets, dirt, and rocks. Their desperate line of defense was now gone, and their house had been gutted by the swiftly moving water.

Just before dark, more dynamite was set off on the river levee, but by then, the creek flood wall was too close to collapsing in several places, and the decision was made to clear out. All would have to wait until first light to see what had happened. Nothing more could be done.

Noisy trucks from the Department of Transportation and National Guard raced away to higher ground. The remainder of the crews, some crying in despair and frustration, and others angry, retreated to see what the morning would bring. Dave Mosely was the last to leave the danger area. As he pulled out, what he saw in the rear view mirror of his truck hit him hard.

Someone had jammed a flagpole into the middle of the creek flood wall, and the American flag gently flapped in the summer night's breeze.

Dave's jaw was tight. "We might have been defeated here, but we didn't quit. We gave it all we had."

*  *  *

Silas Hobart opened his large hilltop home on the hill to the flood workers. With four bedrooms, a full basement, and a large family and living room, he had the space. Kathy prevailed on Jeff and Sandy to stay there that night as well. Jeff and Silas still had some unfinished business, but they kept out of it for now, a silent truce between them.

The twins hardly left Kathy's bedside, where she had not been able to leave since Jeff had brought her back earlier in the day. Silas had called a doctor in the county, and he had promised to be there within the hour. That had been several hours ago and there was still no sign of him.

Natalie had taken it upon herself to watch over Scooter and make sure he got some food in his belly.

"You have to eat something." The little boy looked up at her with hollow eyes. Ever since his first emotional outbreak when the motel had washed away, he had neither spoken nor cried.

Sandy finally wrapped Scooter in a warm blanket, then cradling him in her arms, sat back in a rocking chair and began softly singing to him. Watching anxiously, Natalie bit her lip, worried for the little guy. She knew what it was like to lose someone you deeply loved.

A few minutes later, Raymond Floyde knocked on the front door. When Jeff answered, and Raymond saw Scooter in the chair with Sandy, he motioned Jeff outside.

"There's still no word on the boy's parents. I suppose they might have been washed ashore somewhere and no one has found them yet. Considering the current now, that would take a miracle. We may never find them." Raymond rubbed his face. "So, how's he doing?"

Jeff shook his head. "He hasn't said anything since the incident. Sandy said he was already pulling into himself before she even told him they were dead. It was like he already knew he was alone."

Raymond was so tired his legs trembled. He shook himself to try to wake up. "I have a favor to ask you. Normally, I'd get the boy to the Illinois Social Services. With everything going on here, you can see why I can't right now. So do you suppose you and Sandy could look after him for a while?"

"I don't even know if I have a house anymore."

"I think having *someone* is more important for the little guy than having *somewhere.*"

Jeff agreed. "Yeah, okay. I don't think anyone could get him away from Sandy right now anyway. I've seen that look in her eyes before."

As Raymond walked out to his patrol car, he met John coming up the drive. From where the two of them stood, they had a clear view down the hill to the town, the creek flood wall, and the Mississippi River.

"You could use some sleep, Deputy," said John. Then he yawned so wide he felt his jaws would dislocate.

"Look . . ." the yawning caught Raymond, and he gave in to one of his own. "Look who's talking? You don't look all that fresh yourself."

They both leaned back up against the patrol car and stared at the creek flood wall down below. The last little bit of sunset was fading fast. Soon everything would be dark.

"Come dawn we can see if there's anything left of our town." Raymond sighed, yawning again.

"Yeah, well, it's still a few hours until then, and everyone has done all they can. Go to bed," insisted John.

"One more check down below," declared Raymond. "That's all I have left in me."

"Okay," said John, "but I get to keep you company."

Raymond and John took a small boat and looked around the town again, but this time everyone was gone. Too tired to do anything else, they split up and went their separate ways. By midnight the two men were finally asleep. Both had prayed before they fell into slumber. One got a clear answer on what the morrow would bring, and the other received a deep, comforting sense of peace and hope. He didn't understand it, but was grateful nonetheless.

\* \* \*

Just after two in the morning, Thursday, August 5, Jeff was sitting on a chair near the foot of Kathy's bed. Exhausted, the twins had long been asleep. Silas finally collapsed in his own bed, worn out from worrying about Kathy. The doctor had called, explaining he'd been stopped by emergencies, and was unable to get there until the morning. What he had told Silas about the likely progression of Kathy's illness didn't help.

As she slipped into the room, Sandy whispered to Jeff, "How come you're still up? I thought you were sacked out with the twins."

"They snore too loud."

Sandy grinned and gently gave his shoulder an affectionate squeeze. "Oh, really? Look who's talking! You sound like a freight train sometimes."

"Maybe, but I'm asleep when it's going on. So I don't hear it."

Sandy moved over to the side of the bed and reached out to gently lay her hand across Kathy's forehead. "She's so cold."

"I suppose it won't be long now," said Jeff softly.

Sandy sat on the bed beside Kathy, tucking in the blankets so they better covered her. "I wish there were more we could do for her," she said as she brushed a lock of Kathy's hair away from her face. "I can see why you loved her. She has a good heart. Too bad I couldn't have known her longer."

John appeared in the doorway of the room. He smiled at the two of them and spoke quietly, "Jeff, I'd like to give Kathy a blessing. I just administered to Silas. He's suffering from what looks like pneumonia—his lungs are congested, and he's running a high fever. He wants to help me, but he's very weak. He can't stand for long on his own, but he's insistent on being with his daughter during these last moments of her life. I know things have been rough between you two, but he needs your help. I can't offer the blessing and help Silas at the same time. You need to help him stand while he gives his daughter this one last blessing.

"I can't," Jeff protested hollowly, then stopped and looked from John to Sandy. He slowly lowered his head and gave a small nod. After all these years, he'd finally support Silas—literally. He left and returned a few minutes later with a frail-looking Silas leaning heavily against him as they walked.

John had been explaining exactly what giving a blessing meant in the LDS faith, but stopped talking as the two men entered the room.

After helping Silas get settled in a chair to rest for a moment, John softly said, "I think we'd better wait a minute to let Silas get his bearings. I think it would be a good idea for us to offer a prayer before we begin. Jeff, would you do the honors?"

"It's been too long, I don't remember what to say."

"It's like riding a bike; you never really forget."

Jeff sighed, looked out the window for a moment at the sparkling, starlit night, and made one last effort to get out of it. "I don't know if I'm even worthy to pray anymore."

"I think there is nothing God wants more than to hear you, His own child, pray to Him."

Again Jeff gave a subtle nod. He, John, and Sandy kneeled together near the bed and Silas's chair.

Jeff could feel the knot in his throat tighten. He tried to speak, but it came out almost as a sob as he uttered the words, "Our Father, who art in heaven . . ." Instantly he felt a warmth in his heart he hadn't felt for a very long time. He felt as though the weight that had been resting on his shoulders and chest were suddenly lifted. He hadn't even noticed how heavy it had been until it was gone. His words continued steadily after that, but still trimmed with deep emotion. He thanked his Heavenly Father for the time they had on earth, for the strength of families, and for their Savior. He almost lost his voice as he asked for Kathy to be comforted, and Silas, and the twins. Then, strained with emotion, his voice uttered a plea of forgiveness for his past action. As he closed the prayer, he turned to Sandy and held her tightly. They both knelt and cried softly in the moonlight that poured through the window. They cried all the tears that had been bottled up for so long, at last letting out the stifled emotions of so many years of heartache and loneliness.

At last, when their emotions were more under control, Jeff stood and offered his hand to Silas. Together they walked the few steps to Kathy's bedside.

"You can anoint, and I'll seal," John said to Silas.

Jeff felt the old man shaking as he carefully put one small drop of olive oil on the crown of Kathy's head. He didn't know if it was from the man's illness or the emotion of the hour. After handing the vial back to John, Silas laid his hands on Kathy's head, and feebly but lovingly uttered the words of the blessing.

Then together, John and Silas laid their hands on Kathy's head while Jeff stood close by, supporting his weak ex-father-in-law for the first time ever. After sealing the anointing, John expressed the Lord's deep love for His dying daughter, and His awareness of her repentant heart and service to others. After a brief pause, he seemed to gather his thoughts, then continued with more strength. He told her that her life rested in her Heavenly Father's hands, and then released her from the sorrows of her pain and mortality.

Even as the men withdrew their hands, Kathy's spirit was leaving. Her body relaxed, and she smiled in her sleep, suddenly looking years younger. Her breathing was no longer troubled. Silas bent over and kissed her cheek. "Until we meet again, princess." He let out a sob as his legs gave way and he nearly collapsed in Jeff's arms. Jeff and John eased him back to his chair.

Sandy, sitting as unobtrusively as possible in her chair near the door, marveled at how the room seemed filled with a *presence* of peace, a warm feeling of such deep love that it was nearly tangible. It was a feeling she had witnessed only one other time: at her husband's deathbed. She marveled again at the beauty death seemed to bring, or at least, a death filled with love, such as this father and daughter had been blessed with. Kathy sighed one last time. Her fingers relaxed and fell open lifelessly. Jeff broke down and wept, and Sandy rose to comfort and hold him.

The old man continued to weep from his core, having lost not only his wife but also his daughter. Sandy left Jeff to go hold Silas and mourn with him.

Shortly after that, John left the room and the house. Walking down the driveway of Silas Hobart's home, John set his direction for the town below. The course of many lives would be decided there today. He needed to be part of it.

# chapter 15

In the predawn light, Raymond Floyde drove up in his patrol car to the crest of the hill where John was sitting. Even as the undersheriff came over, John's gaze stayed focused down on the creek flood wall.

"I can't tell yet. Too dark for my poor old eyes. What do *you* see?" asked Raymond.

"It's still there," answered John.

Within five minutes, Raymond could clearly see for himself. The creek flood wall was still there. And the town was no more flooded than it had been the day before. Using his binoculars, Raymond scanned the creek flood wall.

"The water is right to the top. There can't be one inch to spare."

Dave Mosely arrived next, guided by an unseen hand to the same viewpoint. "We held it together, didn't we?"

Raymond handed Dave the binoculars.

"Alright, alright! We did it! Thank God, we won something."

"I do," said John, still sitting on the grass nearby.

Dave slowly lowered the binoculars. "Yeah, thanks be to God. No one else could have saved this town."

\* \* \*

Meanwhile, Sandy was trying to comfort Silas. The doctor had left just an hour before. He had been apologetic and explained that a typhus outbreak demanded his attention, but he ended his visit by treating Silas's pneumonia and calling the funeral home in the county seat to come and get Kathy's body. A long drive to be sure, but everywhere else was flooded out.

"I'm alone, all alone now," moaned Silas.

Sandy wasn't having much luck getting him to take the medicine the doctor had left. Frustrated, she set the bottle down gently on the sink. "Silas, what about your faith in God? That's what you told me I needed when Adam and Robbie died."

Silas shook his head. "No matter what I tried to do, it wasn't enough. They're still dead, and I'm alone."

Scooter was standing in the doorway of the room, watching. Since yesterday he hadn't let Sandy out of his sight for very long, except for her time with Kathy the night before—he had even slept in Sandy's arms.

The boy hunched his shoulders, his eyes getting moist. Then he went around Sandy to the other side of the bed, and climbed in next to Silas. At first Sandy thought she should gently remove him, but then felt something prompt her not to.

"I'm all alone too," said Scooter. "My mom and Mike are gone." These were his first words since the tragedy. "Guess we both need Jesus." Scooter took Silas's hand in his own small one and looked earnestly into the old man's eyes. "John told me that no matter what, I'd never be really alone, because Jesus is always there with me." Scooter's eyes overflowed with tears. "So that means *you* aren't alone either, see? And if we are friends to each other, then we're kind of family too, 'cause they say at church we're all brothers and sisters, right?"

Silas looked upon the little face. How could he compare his loss to this innocent boy's? Silas had enjoyed a lifetime of tremendous personal, family, and professional rewards. What had Scooter been through in his short young life but one trouble after another? And here was this sweet young child, trying to bring *him* comfort!

Silas slipped an arm around Scooter and squeezed. "You're right, Scooter," said Silas, his voice a whisper. "We always have God. Thanks for reminding me." Silas looked up at Sandy and nodded. Scooter grinned and hugged Silas right back.

Sandy's heart felt ready to burst.

Excusing herself, she went out and found Jeff sitting on the back deck. He was staring down at the flooded river valley where their house might, or might not, still be.

"Hold me?" she asked.

"It's going to be okay," he said, pulling her onto his lap.

"Yeah," she answered. "We can put the farm back together when the water goes down."

"No, I didn't mean that. I was talking about us and the kids." He sighed deeply. "And Kathy and Silas and Robbie."

At the mention of Robbie, Sandy looked up into his face, seeing a different light in it.

"I had a dream about him this morning," said Jeff. "Didn't sleep much last night, maybe an hour. Robbie came to me."

"What did the dream mean to you?"

"No, Sandy, Robbie *came*. He was *really here*." Tears formed in Jeff's eyes. "He . . . wanted to tell me . . . he said he loved me. And he forgave me for everything. He told me to stop blaming myself, that blaming was wrong and could never make anything right. He said what I had done didn't kill him. I could almost feel his arms around me, hugging me."

Jeff shook his head. "I . . . I've been so stupid. I'm so sorry for hurting him, and you, and . . ."

Sandy and Jeff held each other tightly as his shoulders shook from sobbing. His eyes held no more tears now, while hers let the tears flow freely.

\* \* \*

John was still sitting in the same place. Raymond and Dave had left to take a boat and inspect the fragile creek flood wall.

Jeff, Sandy, Natalie, and Scooter arrived an hour later, the two kids riding in the back of the pickup, the wind whistling through their hair.

Scooter ran over and gave John a big hug.

"How ya doing, sport?" asked John.

"I miss my mom and Mike."

"Yeah, I know. You'll see them again. I have something for you." John pulled something out of his pocket. It was about the size of Scooter's fist and was wrapped in a paper towel.

Scooter could hardly wait as John pulled away enough of the wrapping to reveal a glass dolphin. The boy's eyes grew wide. "That was my mom's. I gave that to her for her birthday last year."

"Yes you did. And she loved it, because it came from you." John handed it to Scooter. "I thought you might like to keep it for now."

Natalie knelt beside Scooter. The two of them carefully handled the little dolphin figurine as John rose to speak with Jeff and Sandy.

"He's going to need a lot of love to get through this; otherwise he'll just close up again." John looked pointedly at Jeff, who understood and nodded. "And we know how poorly that goes, don't we?"

Sandy smiled over at Scooter. "I . . . we'll look after him. Yesterday something happened with him and Silas . . . there's something about him, that child . . . I don't know what. I feel like he belongs with us now." She looked up at Jeff. He looked down into her eyes and nodded his agreement.

John winked at Jeff and touched Sandy's hand.

"Good, then I won't worry about him. Scooter will look after all of you too. Oh, and Jeff, thanks for trying to help the calf."

Sandy frowned, wondering.

With one last hug for Scooter and a soft whisper to Natalie, John walked down the hill toward the creek flood wall.

"What calf?" Sandy finally asked.

Jeff shrugged. "Yesterday there was a calf caught in the flood. I, uh, I tried to help."

Sandy patted his arm. "That's my hero."

"It was too far gone by the time I got there. I got it up on shore, but it didn't make it."

Sandy said, "Yeah, but you tried. At least you tried." She reached up and kissed his cheek. "That's why you're my hero."

* * *

No one saw John again after that. Unless you count the couple who tried to get back to their submerged home. Those people claimed a man appeared out of nowhere, without a boat, and helped them get unstuck. They had gone inside their house and tried to pull out a prized chest of drawers when a wall collapsed on them.

The stranger, someone with longish brown hair, wearing jeans and a chambray shirt with the sleeves partially rolled up, was able to pull them out to safety. Before they were settled back in their boat and could get his name, he had disappeared.

Then there was a report from one of Raymond Floyde's deputies. He swore that twenty-five miles south of Hampton Corner, just before the tiny village of Cora, someone matching John's description had resuscitated a woman who had drowned trying to save her children. The woman, a single mother, had tried to take her car across a flooded bridge when her car stalled out. The car was stuck in deep water on the bridge for almost half an hour. Then the current took the car with the woman and her children inside, and in moments it disappeared under the water.

The kids somehow surfaced, and rescuers were able to pull them all to safety, but the woman was gone.

Raymond's deputy reported seeing this guy suddenly come wading out of the swollen currents quite a ways downstream with the woman in his arms. He carefully laid her down on the ground, then put his hands on her head and said what looked to be a prayer. Immediately the woman choked up river water and sat up. As rescue workers rushed to check her out the man had disappeared.

For anyone who knew John, his disappearance would be no surprise. That was John's way. As soon as troubles were well enough in hand, and people were on their way to learning what they needed to, he moved on.

As for the flood water, by Sunday the level against the Hampton Creek flood wall dropped by nearly five feet as the holes in the river levee did their job. The Mississippi River had thrown itself many times against the puny, man-made walls, and in most cases it won. Hampton Corner was one fight it didn't win.

# e p i l o g u e

A few weeks later, after the crisis had settled down somewhat, Raymond Floyde found himself receiving a special citation from the county commission for his efforts during the flood. He was uncomfortable with the recognition and said, "I didn't do anything anyone else wasn't doing," but even his boss, the usually conservative Sheriff Pete Picou, insisted Raymond take the award.

"You're going to be my replacement," declared Pete. "It's time for me to hand over the reins to someone else. I've got a lot of fishing to catch up on. And frankly, Raymond, you did a heck of a good job holding this town together. Nobody can deny it. Nobody but a fool would *try* to, if you get my meaning." At that Raymond blushed and gave in.

Dave Mosely quit his job with the Army Corps of Engineers. His experience during the flood had soured his attitude about "taming" the river. In time he became part of a consulting group for natural resource management. His area of specialty became working *with* the river in maintaining and reclaiming wetlands and river plain areas.

Silas Hobart never regained his health. A year later he died and was laid to rest beside his wife and child. Sandy and Scooter made sure to set flowers on the family plot the first Sunday of every month.

The bodies of Mike and Scooter's mother were found washed up on the bank some eleven miles downstream. Sandy and Jeff made sure Mike and Linda had a decent burial and there were many in town who attended the funeral. The young couple had made more friends than anyone had realized with their quiet caring within the community. They were people Scooter could be proud of all of his life.

Scooter never made it into the Illinois State Social Services system of foster care homes. Sandy wouldn't let Scooter out of her life. When she saw the little guy driving the tractor with Jeff, she knew her inspiration about him becoming part of their family was right. They were able to legally adopt Scooter sixteen months later, after they received word that there was no trace of his father, and that he had no other living relatives.

A year after the flood Jeff was called to be elders quorum president, and Sandy, Natalie, and the twins were baptized.

As time passed, the oldest twin, Jason, decided he wanted to design computer games. Surprisingly, Jason's staunchest supporter was his dad. Jarod found he was better at being a farmer than he had thought. He came up with a method to increase the efficiency of feeding hogs that also decreased the amount of time needed to feed them. He also discovered a new feed formula that was so effective he planned to market it. And it was his hog that won grand champion at the county fair the next summer.

\* \* \*

Two years after the flood, on the anniversary of Robbie's death, a package arrived at the MacFarland farm. It sat on the kitchen table all day after the UPS driver delivered it. There was no return address except for the name "John." The driver could only tell them it had been sent from France.

That evening, after dinner, the family gathered around the package.

"Now?" asked Jeff.

"Now," said Sandy.

Inside were several individually wrapped packages. One of them was a crystal dolphin that matched the one Scooter loved so much.

Natalie got an autographed, first edition, hardback copy of *Dandelion Wine* by Ray Bradbury. Inside, the inscription read:

*Best wishes to my loyal reader.*
— *Ray Bradbury*

The twins each got a can of French candy that they lost no time in eating. Jeff received a copy of a Scottish Church record that filled in long lost holes in the MacFarland family history. Folded carefully inside it was a note.

*Jeff, I thought this would help you get going on your family history work. And I have it on good authority that Robbie has accepted the gospel.*

Jeff was beginning to have his suspicions about who "John" was. He noticed Sandy couldn't speak when she opened her gift. "What's wrong, sweetheart?"

The kids had moved off into other rooms, but Sandy motioned Jeff to follow her out onto the front porch. "Here," she said, "read it out loud."

"Dear Sandy," read Jeff, "you were the hardest to find something for. I knew by now you would feel you had everything your heart could expect on this earth. Well, you're wrong. It took me a while to get this, but here it is. Enjoy."

"What did you get?" Asked Jeff. "I didn't see anything else in the box." Sandy slowly opened her hand. There, in her palm, was a small, silver-framed triptych photograph set. Sandy, Jeff, and their family were on one side. Mike, Linda, and Scooter were on the other, and a picture of the temple was between them.

"I think John is hinting at something," she said, her eyes smiling.

Jeff and Sandy looked at each other and knew what the photos meant. They had talked about going to the temple, but had not yet followed through. "We *have* to go, now," said Jeff. "We have to do our work, and theirs, and get started on the family files."

Sandy smiled widely at him. Where had her loveable grump gone? No matter. It was where they were going that mattered.

\* \* \*

Even as Sandy and Jeff were planning to become an eternal family in Illinois, John was digging around an olive tree in Greece. The old couple who owned the grove wouldn't have minded. Since John had shown up, the fading olive groves had come back to life.

At that moment the sun came out from behind a cloud. Birds sang happily as if to welcome it. Not far away a group of dark-haired children were coming home from a local school. Visiting with John had become something they looked forward to. But not as much as he did. John smiled as he dug the shovel in one more time.

Other times he would be somewhere else. There would always be other missions to fulfill. For now though, he was content. No one had to convince him to leave the future in God's hands. After all, John had been doing that for a long, long time.

---

[1] "Do not go gentle into that good night . . . " Is the first line and title of a poem by Dylan Thomas that addresses fighting against old age and death.

[2] Luke 9:55—56.

[3] John 16:33

[4] John 14: 26

[5] John 14:27

[6] 1 Corinthians 13

## about the author

THOMAS ENO is a lover of word games, trivia, practical jokes, and a good pun. He is a mental health therapist who specializes in the healing of trauma victims. A passionate believer in the gospel and avid scriptorian, he serves at this time in his favorite calling as a Gospel Doctrine teacher. Tom lives with his wife and three daughters in Southern Utah, where he currently works with troubled teens and their families.

*An excerpt from Kerry Blair's . . .*

# closing in

*He formed many different words, but there was one word he never could manage to form, although he wished it very much. It was the word ETERNITY.*

— *The Snow Queen, Story the Seventh: The Palace of the Snow Queen & What Happened There At Last, 1845*

"Pay careful heed to the beginning of this story," Libby James read aloud, "for when we get to the end of it we shall know more than we do now about love and greed and the ice that can freeze in our hearts."

She read *The Snow Queen*, but Libby's voice was like sunshine and held a promise of romance and mystery that most of the children in this shabby school library would discover only in the pages of the books she brought to life. The kids seated cross-legged on the worn, wooden floor were sixth-graders, and though most of them considered themselves too old for fairy tales, they leaned forward eagerly, basking in the warmth of Libby's smile and entranced by the luster in her wide pewter eyes.

But nobody in the room paid closer attention than their teacher, David Rogers, because nobody had more interest in how a story about greed would turn out. He was a newcomer to this small, predominantly Mormon town, and though he claimed to have come to teach, he had actually been sent to learn—learn, that is, what the beautiful bibliophile "Libby James" was actually up to.

David crossed his arms and leaned one broad shoulder against a bookcase as his gaze slid from the librarian's sleek, honey-colored ponytail down her tanned legs to her sandal-clad feet. Her dress showed taste and style and subtle curves. Her toenails were unpainted, he noted, as were her fingernails and lips. Not that she needed makeup. The glow that the Arizona sun had lent her delicate features was more complimentary than any cosmetic.

Though in person she scarcely resembled the stylish woman in the photographs, David knew that she *was* the suspect from his electronic case files. This Libby James was really Elisabeth Jamison, one of the richest, most powerful women in corporate America. Moreover, she was suspected of selling missile designs to terrorists.

"The story begins with a wicked hobgoblin," Libby told the children in a hushed, mysterious voice. "He was the worst. And he only came out from hiding when he wanted to cause mischief."

Which was, ironically, the opposite of what she'd done, David thought. The "mischief" at Jamison Enterprises—in the form of yet another sale of classified, technology-laden microchips to Iran—had coincided too perfectly with Libby's anonymous arrival in Amen, Arizona to be much of a coincidence. No matter how she told that story, the theme was treason.

"The antagonist in the story is the Snow Queen." Libby cast David a look cool enough to remove his eyes from her legs, at least for the moment. "Though she was made of ice, she was fair and beautiful and her eyes sparkled like bright stars."

She had that part right. Try as he might, it took more self-control than David possessed not to stare at Libby. She was an attractive traitor to her country; he'd have to grant her that.

But Captain Rogers didn't like traitors. It was that prejudice that initiated his covert move from NASA to the CIA and landed him here in yet another episode of "Mission: Improbable." He might be on board a space shuttle right now if not for what he'd seen—and overheard—on the last one. His well-developed sense of honor had taken him from the pilot's chair on the *Endeavor* to the Internal Affairs Center at NASA and from there to a Central Intelligence Agency office in Washington. Sworn in at the CIA, David had gone back to NASA undercover to help crack a major conspiracy.

David hadn't known what to expect after his former shuttle commander was arrested along with two foreign spies. Maybe a congressional medal or citation of valor? He'd wondered if either honor would cause his grandfather, the four-star admiral, to sit up and take notice—as his graduation at the top of his class at Annapolis and assignment to the space program had not. At any rate, David never found out because all he'd been given was another undercover assignment—this time to a godforsaken spot near the suburbs of obscurity.

He looked over his ragtag class and shook his head ruefully. Sure, he'd taken a sacred oath to protect and serve the United States of America—and he'd meant every word of it—but who'd have guessed he'd be asked to do it this way? Babysitting preadolescents while spying on a turncoat with the legs of a goddess and the face of a saint. It was downright funny when he thought about it.

"'One day, when he was in a merry mood,'" Libby read, "'the hobgoblin made a looking-glass which had the power to make everything beautiful that was reflected in it look hideous. The loveliest landscapes looked like boiled spinach, and people?—well, even one freckle on the nose appeared to spread over the whole of the face.'"

The children giggled at the face Libby made and even David grinned.

"This is what?" a man's voice asked quietly from behind him. "A hob—? Hob-gob-lin? You might tell me, please?"

*Omar.* David identified the man without looking.

*Who else?* David had been in town for only a day and a half and already he knew that Amen was not what it seemed. Sure, it *looked* like a little town dying in the desert foothills outside of Phoenix, but it was actually more like a thriving desert island inside the Bermuda Triangle. There must be *some* cosmic undercurrent of weirdness to account for all the misfits who'd washed up here—like this new Egyptian PE coach, for instance.

David turned. "A hobgoblin is a, a . . . " *What the heck is a hobgoblin, anyway?* Fairy tales hadn't been part of his curriculum in military school.

It didn't matter that David didn't know. Omar had turned away to listen intently to Libby's story. *And no wonder*, David thought. The century-old words rolled easily from her tongue and her expressive face told more than the words. She was a natural storyteller. No wonder she was so good at covering her tracks.

"'As the clock in the church tower struck twelve,'" she read, "'the boy Kay said, "Oh! Something has struck my eye!" Sweet Gerda put her arm around his neck and looked into his eyes, but she could see nothing. "I think it is gone," she said. But she was wrong. It was not gone.'"

Libby's expressive face clouded as she continued, "'It was one of those bits of the evil looking-glass. Poor little Kay had received a small grain in his eye, and another in his heart, which very quickly turned to a lump of ice. He felt no more pain, but the glass was there still.'" She closed the book slowly and smiled when the children groaned in disappointment. "It's almost three o'clock," she said, tapping the watch on her slender wrist. "Time to go home."

"But what happens next?" asked a redheaded girl.

"Kay is bewitched by the Snow Queen," Libby replied. "We'll read that chapter when you come back to the library on Wednesday."

The girl's pigtails swung out from her head as she turned toward David. "Can't you read the rest of the story to us in class tomorrow?"

Other kids joined in with "Yeah!" and "Please, Captain Rogers?"

David smiled. No way could he compete with Scheherazade up there, but he *could* read, and he'd had a heck of a time today filling all those hours he was supposed to be teaching. He'd killed most of the time telling stories about NASA, but he hadn't told them well. David was an ace pilot and a passable secret agent, but he was a lousy public speaker. Lecturing, even to eleven-year-olds, unnerved him. The girl's suggestion was a godsend. "Sure, we'll read the story," he told the class. To Libby he said, "Can I use your book?"

Her fingers tightened around the dog-eared pages. At last she said, "You may check it out, I suppose."

*Right,* David thought as she rose to place the book on her desk, *you worry about me stealing fairy tales, and I'll worry about you stealing government secrets.* Still, he couldn't help but admire the way Libby formed his class into an orderly line at the door. A line was a novel concept; he'd brought them to the library in a mob. When the dismissal bell sounded, the children scattered to the seven winds.

David watched them go from the open doorway and let out an involuntary sigh of relief. Anybody who thought that NASA's infamous altitude chamber was the worst place you could spend a day had never been in charge of a sixth-grade classroom. He glanced at his watch and when he looked up he realized that the seven winds hadn't carried the children off after all. Instead, they'd been blown back toward the library with all their little brothers and sisters.

"He *is* an astronaut!" Calvin, a freckle-faced boy at the front of the pack, declared. He peered around David into the library for an unimpeachable witness. "Tell them, Miss James! Captain Rogers is *too* an astronaut, ain't he?"

"Isn't he," Libby corrected automatically. "Well, he *says* he is."

David started in surprise. Then he relaxed. No way was Elisabeth Jamison on to him. Even if she'd had him checked out, and there was no intelligence from headquarters to indicate that she had, at least not yet, his cover was flawless. He *was* an astronaut for crying out loud; he had the scars to prove it.

"I've flown the *Atlantis* and the *Endeavor*," he told the children. "Orbited the earth. Walked in space. The whole nine yards."

"He showed us pictures!" the boy exclaimed. "Let's go show 'em your pictures, Captain Rogers!"

If Calvin had pictures to back him up, the children were willing to believe. One little girl tugged on David's pant leg. "Can I ask you a question about outer space?"

David looked down into the dirty, eager face and smiled. "Sure you can. What do you want to know?"

"Where do you go to the bathroom?"

The group giggled. Behind his back, he heard Libby repeat the question for Omar. Suddenly, he felt his face warm without benefit of the afternoon sun. "We, er, well, the . . . facilities . . . are like a vacuum cleaner kind of thing and you take the hose and—" The laughter increased in volume and David regretted the graphic nature of his explanation. He was grateful to see principal Max Wheeler, a shaggy gray bear of a man, ambling toward the library for the faculty meeting. As one, the children stepped back to let him pass.

"This the organizational meeting of your fan club, Captain?" Before David could respond, a smile lit the older man's craggy features and he added, "Sign me up. Not every school can claim to have a real Buck Rogers on their staff."

David returned the smile as though he hadn't been called "Buck Rogers of the 21st Century" at least once a week since he got his pilot's license at the age of twelve. He was twenty-eight now, so he'd heard it—what—eight hundred times? Nine hundred? *Probably more like a thousand,* he thought, *but hey, something that clever never gets old.* "I'll, uh, show you guys the pictures tomorrow," he told the children as he turned to follow Max back into the library.

"Your book," Libby said when he paused at her desk. The way she extended the volume of fairy tales seemed designed to push him away.

David didn't budge. Instead he flashed his killer grin—the one reserved for NASA Public Affairs photographers and female senators on the Space Committee. He knew he was somewhat attractive, and he wasn't above using his good looks to his advantage. He didn't mind that saving the Free World called for a little flirtation when the flirtee was as lovely as Libby James. He leaned confidently across her desk. "What I'd really like to check out is the librarian."

The look she gave him suggested there was more space between his ears than he'd see in a lifetime at NASA.

*Okay,* he thought, *so it wasn't a great come-on.* He turned the charm up another notch. "What I mean is, can I take you to dinner tonight?"

"No."

The suggestion, he realized at once, was worse than the come-on. There was only one diner in town—The Garden of Eaten—and it had taken David less than two minutes to determine that what its cook lacked in olfactory senses she made up for in poor hygiene. Of course Libby wouldn't want to eat there. Nobody would want to eat there. He tried again. "Can I take you to a movie this weekend?"

"No."

"You've probably seen it." There was only one theater in town too, and it was showing *Camelot*. With his charm already on "high," and his ego on the line, David wondered what *would* be appealing to a woman like Elisabeth Jamison. Then he remembered where they were: Amen, Arizona, where the brightest light of the big city was the 60-watt street light in front of town hall. *No ballet. No symphony. No museum. Heck, there isn't even a bowling alley. What do people here do?*

"Can I walk you to church?" he asked finally. There were two of those. A new chapel anchored Main Street, and an old adobe house of worship—built by the pioneers Brigham Young had first sent to settle Amen—fell to ruin at the edge of town. When she hesitated, David wondered if it would help to "accidentally" flash his temple recommend. He'd already let drop at their introduction that he belonged to the Church.

"No," Libby said.

So much for flirtation. Not only was he not above it, he wasn't good at it. "Okay then." He tucked the library book under his arm. "Maybe I'll see you around school." He retreated before she could say "no" to that too.

As the other six teachers filed in for the meeting, David pulled out a chair next to the PE coach, dropped the fairy tales on the table and frowned at its cover. "You want to know who the *real* Snow Queen is?" he asked Omar under his breath. "It's Libby James over there."

Words spoken in haste are often lamented in leisure. That was the lesson Captain David Rogers would best remember from his first day at Alma Elementary School.